PRAISE ...

A sexy and engaging tale with likable characters who have room to grow.

— KIRKUS REVIEWS

[A] light, touching story of finding and choosing a tribe allows readers to live vicariously through the central heroine's life spent on the road..

— BOOKLIFE PRIZE

Lynda's writing style has always been one of my favorites. She has a unique way of bringing a story to life. This fascinating tale about Abby Steele is simply a joy to read. Abby is easy to relate to in today's modern world. She is definitely not your average "biker chick."

— ZACH M

Steel Journeys captures the heart of an adventurous and independent woman with a thirst for travel and new experiences. I thoroughly enjoyed this relatable read!

— JO JO

Lynda Meyers has done it again! She has captured both my imagination and sense of adventure with her latest novel - Steel Journeys, The Road to Patagonia.

— W.A. Sᴍɪᴛʜ

STEEL JOURNEYS

THE ROAD TO PATAGONIA

LYNDA MEYERS

HALLWAY
11

For all the women out there busting their asses to be the best they can be at whatever it is they do.
I love you all. Don't change a thing.

The Bitches of Steel Mantra

Whatever you do.
Whatever you ride.
However you choose.
Stand tall and with pride.

ACKNOWLEDGMENTS

Every book is a labor of love. This, my fourth book, was birthed in similar fashion to my fourth child. Relatively quickly but with difficulty. Not to mention getting kind of stuck at the end there.

My children have been my whole world for most of my adult life. When they were little, I was always their biggest fan, and now that they're grown, they have all become mine. In writing, and in life, they are always the biggest, most important part of everything I do.

And to Wendel,

Because of your love and support, my life is so much richer. Psst. I love you!

PART I

1

Abby Steel hadn't seen the inside of her own apartment in over three years. There hadn't been any need to come home really, so she just...didn't. Life on the road kept her busy and building her own business had taken way more time and energy than she'd anticipated.

She looked at the compulsively clean apartment and was thankful, once again, that her sister came and dusted the surfaces once a month. It wasn't as if she'd left it dirty, but time and dust had a way of accumulating in equal and inevitable measure. Lauren had also been nice enough to retrieve her mail from the post office when it no longer fit in her box, getting rid of all the junk mail and opening anything that seemed important. There wasn't much. Abby had very few bills outside the business, most of which were handled remotely.

At this point, she was thankful for familiar surroundings and the chance to recharge. Three years was a long time to be away. It was time to reconnect with her roots and what was left of her family. Riding back from Alaska, many miles had been spent dreaming about long showers and luxurious baths with unlimited hot water. The grime that had built up under her fingernails would need to be soaked and scrubbed, her hair untangled and brushed—things life on the road rarely allowed for.

It would be good to see Lauren and her nieces in the flesh, instead of over video chat. She was excited to share stories of her adventures and show off her pictures, but seeing them would have to wait until she had energy for endless questions from curious little girls. She sat down in one of the comfortable side chairs in the living room with a glass of water and a stack of mail, but barely got through half of it before falling asleep.

When she woke up, the sun had dipped below the horizon, shrouding the apartment in a kind of eerie glow that reminded her of sunsets on the Spanish plains just outside Sevilla. She closed her eyes and let the scene linger in her mind, colors bursting across the open sky with the sweltering summer heat billowing up inside her leather jacket. Riding there had been nothing short of magical. A lot of places felt that way.

It was the magic that kept her on the road. Each new place had its own set of challenges, its own set of charms. The challenges faded, but the charms remained, decorating her memories and dangling from her heart.

For Abby, the constant drifting from place to place created an unusual sort of routine that was comforting in its uncertainty. Lauren thought it was crazy, never knowing where she was going to sleep or what dangers might lurk around the corner, but one person's danger is another person's thrill. She and Lauren, they were wired differently, that's all.

California's Napa Valley had been home for thirty-three years, but she left the small-town of Calistoga with an insatiable need not just to see, but to fully experience all the world had to offer. By that time, she'd already seen most of the US, and a good portion of Canada, but those had all been shorter trips—three weeks at most.

Culture shock becomes something of a nonissue when

you're constantly changing cultures. Eventually, the life she'd left in California was no longer the ruler by which she measured all of her other experiences. Instead, her old life became just one of many other foreign concepts, all blended together in a beautiful mélange. Living abroad had changed so many of her perspectives that her old worldview seemed distorted by comparison.

Leaving the confines of the continental United States and choosing to travel the world turned out to be a polarizing decision. Three years later, she felt like a completely different version of herself.

Being back in her apartment, surrounded by all the furniture and artwork she'd left behind was its own sort of culture shock. They were her belongings, of course, but all the things she thought she would miss had eventually faded into the background. They'd been replaced by people, places, smells, and tastes of a life too vibrant and varied to be contained within four walls.

The life she had built before was there on the walls and in the furniture, blended into the color scheme. They defined a person she wasn't sure existed anymore. A part of her recognized it, was even comforted by the deep familiarity, but an even bigger part wondered if it was possible to go back in time. Time seemed to have gone on without her.

Maybe coming home wasn't a matter of choosing now or then, but rather, allowing the new to inform the old, and the old to make space for the new. If her life was a tree, like the sadhu in India had told her, then she could never hope to become a different tree. The new experiences would instead have to be grafted onto the trunk, eventually growing together into a unique expression of life.

Steel Journeys was a company she had founded all on her own, most of the seed money coming from her inheritance. Lauren had used her half to build a house in the suburbs and was raising two beautiful daughters. Abby chose to pay off debt, buy a condo, and set off on the adventure of a lifetime. She'd spent the past three years researching the best roads, the best views, and the best options for lodging in dozens of countries, taking copious notes and pictures, giving out business cards, and forming business relationships.

Cataloging it all had been a labor of love, born of passion and drive. Each new place had its own rugged truths waiting to be discovered. She filled several paper journals with notes and sketches, cross-referenced with digital galleries.

She couldn't recall precisely when the idea for the business hit her—it was somewhere between Bangkok and Ho Chi Minh City. Like a reformed smoker she suddenly, desperately wanted other women like her to experience the freedom she had seen, felt, heard, smelled, and tasted. That was the dream—to form a women's motorcycle touring company and take it global.

"What, the entirety of the United States isn't enough for you?" Lauren had asked.

The answer was simple. It wasn't enough. It would never be enough. Wanderlust was embedded deep in her DNA—so deep, in fact, that she wasn't sure where it ended and she began.

Lauren was happy being a soccer mom and living in the suburbs. She was a card-carrying member of the PTA. The only cards Abby carried were a Visa and her gun permit. She didn't carry her gun internationally, of course, but traveling solo had taught her a thing or two about self-protection. Tucked into remote corners of the globe, far from big cities and police patrols, the rules were different. Street smarts were learned, and she had learned plenty.

It *was* a long time to be away, but for Abby, home was a concept, not a place. To some people, home might be wherever you laid your helmet, but for Abby, home was wherever she laid her ass. Home was her saddle, which for the last three years had been a Harley, and before that a BMW, a Triumph, and a custom café racer she'd rebuilt with her dad. Home was the wind in her face and wide-open spaces tucked under an expansive sky.

Home was the road.

This homecoming—this apartment—was one more stop along the way. It was the obligatory reset point on a map filled with pushpins. Except, of course, this room was tastefully decorated, with a comfortable bed, down blankets, and the best sheets money could buy. That bed was calling to her, and the rest would have to wait.

She woke the next morning with dirt on the sheets and little balls of dirt surrounding her jeans, which were hastily removed and crumpled up in the corner like a one-night stand. Perhaps a shower might have been the better choice before bed, but it was still a hundred times cleaner than most of the places she'd lived recently. Dirt was a part of life, and the only thing it damaged was a person's sense of expectation. She put it out of her mind and padded toward the bathroom.

The requisite extra-long shower, complete with a double scrubbing of her hair, ears, fingernails, and feet took longer than strictly necessary. Lauren was expecting her, but after three years, what was another thirty minutes? When she felt reasonably satisfied with her results, she filled the bathtub with lavender-scented Epsom salts and soaked, with the sun streaming through the glass block window.

As she soaked, she listened to pan flutes and meditation music that reminded her of some of the temples and monasteries she'd visited in India. She only spent a few weeks there, barely scratching the surface of just one region, and there was still so much to see and explore. Indian people were very kind to her, and she admired their deep spirituality. It was definitely on her *must-return* list.

She emerged from the bath and pulled a long, clean, white T-shirt and some yoga pants out of the closet. "Well hey there, guys! I haven't seen you in forever!" She paused for a moment, staring at the sheer volume of clothing neatly arrayed before her and shook her head. After surviving for so long on two perpetually wrinkled shirts and one tank top, it all seemed so extra.

Still, it felt amazing not to be wearing jeans or leathers, and *not* sweating into a helmet for a couple of hours was a delicious thought. Most of the time she wore her thick brown hair up or braided to keep it out of her face. She decided to blow it out a little and let the ends curl up naturally with some leave-in conditioner. She'd barely noticed how long it had become. Upon closer inspection, it was desperately in need of a trim, but split ends would have to wait.

Life's sense of urgency was something that had mellowed over the miles. Time was slower in other parts of the world. Life was about the experience. Relationships. Good conversations. Being present in the now was something she was still working on, but an area where she'd seen a hell of a lot of improvement.

It was satisfying to think that some measure of growth and change and wisdom had come over time. Everything had fallen into place, and she was finally doing exactly what she wanted with her life. When she opened the back door to let in some fresh air, even the birds sounded happy. The way the morning was going, nothing could harsh her mellow.

Except maybe her ex-boyfriend showing up at her door.

2

_____

When the knock sounded, she figured it might be Lauren and the girls—too excited to wait. Instead, it was Trevor, and fifteen years evaporated in less than fifteen seconds. Damn if he wasn't still just as fine as she remembered.

"What the hell are you doing here?" Behind him was a shiny black Gold Wing, leaned over on its kickstand. It was a newer version of the bike they had ridden up into Canada and down through Glacier National Park.

That was before she rode her own. Back when he was the sweet guy who taught her how to ride and fix her own bike. Back before he got hammered one night and fucked her best friend in a hayfield.

He _claimed_ he didn't remember doing it, but in those days, blackouts were his specialty. Whether they were the sign of a real problem or just an excuse was anybody's guess. They were just kids then. She was barely twenty-one when it ended.

It had been well over fifteen years since she'd seen or heard anything from him, and it shouldn't have mattered anymore, but it did. He was still having trouble keeping those loose, defiant curls out of his eyes. Standing there in his signature faded jeans and white T-shirt, with just enough stubble to be irritatingly sexy, he looked like the ghost of Christmas past.

Trevor was always lean, but a little on the squishy side, what with all the beer and whiskey he consumed. She wondered if he still drank at all, given the way his muscles rippled under that T-shirt. He was tan too.

"Where've you been? The Caribbean?"

He smiled at the edge in her tone. "Close. Florida, actually."

She tried not to imagine him in a pair of swim trunks lying on a beach. If only he would say something. Anything. An explanation, perhaps, of what the *hell* he was doing on her porch?

"That yours?" He inclined his head to indicate her Harley, which was now snuggled up to his Gold Wing.

"That's right."

"She's awful dirty." He smiled. "Where've you been ridin'?"

"Perú, Croatia, Greenland. But most recently, Alaska..."

"Wait—seriously?"

"Yes. Seriously." Men were always so incredulous about her solo travel, and it was annoying as fuck. "I just got back last night. How did you even know I was here?" She linked her arms across her chest and waited.

He looked confused. As if he didn't understand the question.

"Trev!"

He looked at her face, trying, it seemed, to find his tongue.

"What are you doing here?"

He seemed almost embarrassed, which was totally unlike him. "Can I come in for minute?"

Abby had been in more dangerous situations than this, she was sure of it, but at the moment she couldn't remember any. Trevor was her first love—her first everything. He was goddamned quicksand.

Against her better judgment, she swung the door wide and

motioned for him to come in. As he walked by, she caught his scent and it all came flooding back. Late nights hanging out behind the pizza place where he worked, making love in random fields on a blanket he kept in one of his saddlebags... They used to lie on their backs looking up at the stars, talking about all the things they wanted to do together. All the places they wanted to go. Suddenly, going back out on the road felt like a pretty good option.

"Wow. This is a really nice place." Trevor peeked into the living room. "I like how open it feels."

"Thanks. I'd forgotten how much I liked it myself. I haven't been here in about three years."

"What do you mean you haven't been here in three years?"

"I told you, I've been traveling."

"For three years? Straight?" One eyebrow tipped up as his face registered the shock. Whoever had told him where she lived obviously hadn't shared much else. "You mean you didn't come home at all?"

"What is *home*? Is it a place where your shit lives? No." She shook her head. "Home is where I say it is. Today it's here, but tomorrow it might not be."

He looked down and ran his fingers through his hair. "Same old Abby. You never could sit still."

The sitting still part might be true, but she wasn't the same old Abby. She had changed so much over the past fifteen years. She couldn't even begin to tell him how much, but that was beside the point entirely.

She walked toward the kitchen and he followed her. "Are you going to tell me what you're doing here, or am I supposed to guess?"

Trevor stuffed his hands in his pockets and looked at his shoes for a long time before he spoke. "I have a daughter, Abby."

"Congratulations. And this concerns me...how?"

"With Claire."

Ok, that one stung. Her first response kind of stuck in her throat, and it was probably best to leave it there. It was too early for spewing obscenities, so she decided on something slightly more civilized. "I assume you mean Claire, my former best friend? The one you slept with before conveniently blacking out the entire experience? Yes, I remember her." Abby wasn't about to show an ounce of emotion for that situation. Her tears had been spent on him a long time ago. "How is dear sweet Claire anyway?"

"She's dead." Trevor said the words as if he didn't believe them.

Her sarcasm fell away for a moment. Abby didn't know what to say. "She's what?"

"She died—about a month ago. Maybe more, I'm not sure. Time is all mashed together at the moment. It's not really making sense yet."

"I'm sorry." Abby tried to sound sincere, but this was Claire they were talking about, and truth be known she'd wished her dead a thousand times since that night. The venom in her heart rose up and mingled with years of festering anger.

"Yeah. Me too. She was a good mother. She loved Kelsey. And me too, God knows why."

You poor, brokenhearted bastard. Did he actually think the grieving widower bit was working? She imagined Trevor trying to be a single dad to a little girl in pigtails, teaching her the only skills he knew well—like taking apart a carburetor on an old Honda. Abby imagined her first words being things like throttle and kickstand, and her heart softened a little. "How old is Kelsey?"

"She's fifteen." The look on his face cut through the bullshit with an undeniable truth.

"She's—"

"Yes."

Abby took a couple of steps back from him instinctively. The world started to go black, and she put her hand on the table to keep from falling over.

"Are you ok?" He moved toward her, but she put her hand up to stop him.

"I'm fine." She cleared her throat and stood a little straighter. "I'm sorry for your loss."

"Abby—"

Suddenly, spewing obscenities felt like a fine choice. "What the hell do you want me to say, Trevor? You didn't have the balls to tell me this fifteen years ago, so why now? I'm going to ask you one more time. *Why* are you here?"

"I moved back home. With Kelsey. Claire's parents are still here, my parents are still here, and hell, I don't know anything about raising a teenage girl. Frankly it scares the living shit out of me."

"What does that even mean? You haven't been in her life at all?"

"In and out. It's kind of a long story."

She glanced at the clock on the stove, then inclined her head toward the door. "Yes well, I'm due at Lauren's soon so I'm afraid—"

"I've been working on getting my act together," he finished.

"For fifteen years? We're in our thirties, Trev. You kind of need to have that part figured out."

"You think I don't know that?"

It was like they were right back in their old routine, and it was grating on her nerves. "So...what's the plan?"

"My dad's giving me another chance at a job."

"In an *office*?" Abby laughed out loud. "I see. So you came to borrow a rope and a stool?"

"I *asked* for the job. I want to run the business someday."

"But that's not you."

"I'm good at building things—and fixing things."

Except relationships. She shook her head. "You'd go crazy at a desk job."

"What do you know about me, Abby? We haven't seen each other in almost sixteen years. I went back to school."

"For your GED?"

"No, for my MBA."

"Your..." This conversation had gone from terrible to ridiculous. It was Abby's turn to run her fingers through her hair. Nothing made sense. She couldn't line the pieces up the right way. "Would you like a cup of coffee? I haven't had any coffee yet and this conversation seems to require more brainpower than I currently possess."

"That'd be nice. Thanks."

She moved past him, and his nostrils flared.

"Man, you smell good. What is that?"

"Soap." Abby rolled her eyes. "I forgot about that nose of yours. You were always so sensitive to smells. Never got over that, huh?" She motioned for him to sit down as she rifled through the cupboard. "Have a seat. I hope instant is ok. I'll be surprised if there's anything else here. We're both kind of taking our chances."

"Anything is fine. Thanks." He took a seat as directed.

She pulled two cups down and filled them from the instant hot water dispenser. When she bought the place, having one felt so necessary. Now it just felt over the top.

"Can I ask you something?"

She set the cups on the counter. *This ought to be good.* "Go ahead."

"Why would you pay rent on a place if you knew you'd be gone for three years straight?"

"Well, Mr. MBA, I don't pay rent. I bought this. Outright. After my parents died."

His eyes got wide. "Your parents died? Both of them? When?"

Abby stirred the packets into the water and handed him the coffee.

When their hands touched, he looked up, nodding with an understanding that defied logic.

"Oh, right!"

"Excuse me?"

"Your parents. Three years ago, right?" He shrugged. "Hell, I would've hit the road too."

"I see you also took classes in clairvoyance. Was that a minor?" The fact that he could dissect her choices so accurately was irritating.

He shook his head and sipped his coffee. "Same old Abby."

"Stop saying that, would you? I am *not* the same old Abby. I've been all over the world. I've seen and done things I never thought possible."

"And yet..." He took another sip of coffee. "Here we are, both thinking we know all there is to know about the other person."

She laughed at the truth of his statement and raised her cup. "Guilty."

He returned the salute. "Truce?"

It was much too early for a truce. She took a long drink of too-hot coffee and stared into her cup, contemplating her next words. "Why didn't you tell me? About the baby?"

He swallowed hard. "I couldn't. I don't know why."

"Did you marry her?" She didn't mean to ask the question out loud, but somehow it slipped out. She braced herself for the answer.

He shook his head. "We tried to stay together at first, for Kelsey's sake, but it just never worked. It was never right. Not that first night. Not ever."

"Well, you're right about that first night." She leaned back.

He shifted uncomfortably in his seat. "I tried to stay in Kelsey's life, but for a long time I didn't know what I wanted.

Eventually I went back to school. About five years ago, Claire was diagnosed with cancer. She didn't even tell me until she got really sick. She beat it that first time—and the second. It just kept coming back in different places."

Cry me a river. It wasn't that Abby was cold-hearted. A kid orphaned at fifteen was no laughing matter, but still—hell hath no fury and all...

"You look good, Abby. The road's been good to you."

She rolled her eyes, thankful for both the lavender and the blow dryer. "You should have smelled me yesterday. I hadn't had a bath in over a month. Or a real shower, unless you count water crossings through frigid streams in the Alaskan wilderness."

"How the fuck did you ride a Harley through Alaska?" He grinned.

"I didn't. I rented a BMW for that part. Picked the Harley back up in Anchorage."

"How did you like it?"

"I've ridden them quite a bit, but yeah I love that bike. The GS has become my new favorite dual sport. It's so versatile." Why the hell was she talking to him as if they were friends who chatted about the merits of different bikes? She cleared her throat.

"Why?"

"Why what?"

"Why Alaska?"

Why *anywhere?* The question itself was so tedious. There were so many reasons, none of which she felt like explaining. "Denali."

"Oh, man." He shook his head. "I've heard amazing things about Denali."

"All true. Even saw a grizzly."

"No shit?"

When he grinned, she saw the smile of the kid she fell in

love with and it speared her. "No shit." She swirled the coffee in her cup. "Instant sure has come a long way since we were kids. Remember that swill we used to drink?"

"In the orange packets? To stay awake all night—yes!" He laughed. "Man, that was some nasty-ass shit."

"I've had worse." She tried crossing her legs, but that felt too ladylike, so she leaned back and let her knees fall open but then closed them up again. She sighed, looking at the clock. She didn't have time for small talk, and she didn't feel like traipsing down memory lane either, despite the current obvious exception. "What are you going to do now?"

Trevor shrugged again. "Make a life? Try to raise Kelsey as best I can. She's a good kid, Abby. You'd like her."

"Have you taught her how to ride yet?"

"Her mother forbade it." He downed the last of his coffee, although how he could stand it that hot was beyond her comprehension.

Abby wondered why Claire would forbid something like that, and the silence hung between them. "You could have just called. Why did you come?"

He didn't answer right away. "I wanted to see you."

"Why?" She looked straight into his eyes and he stared back, the packed-up memories unfolding in the space between them.

"You know why."

She got up and put her cup in the sink. "I don't even have words to tell you how many things are wrong with that statement. That ship sailed a long, long time ago."

"It's not like that. I just need a friend."

"Call Jim Beam."

"He and I aren't on speaking terms anymore."

She spun toward him, held up one hand, and started counting on her fingers. "Clean-cut. Sober. Father to a motherless child. MBA." She shook her head, wiggling her thumb. "The prodigal returns."

He stood and moved closer, taking her hands and closing her splayed fingers into a fist. "I'm sorry I hurt you, Abby. I know it took me a long time to tell you that. Too long. I tried to do the right thing. I'm still trying."

He was dangerously close to her face, and she couldn't think straight. As his eyes traced her lips, she remembered his tongue and the way his kisses used to feel along her neck. He wasn't playing fair.

Trevor took a step back, pulled a card out of his pocket, and laid it on the table. "Thanks for letting me in. I'm sorry I didn't call first, but I didn't have your number." He kissed her cheek. His lips were soft and they lingered a second too long. "I'll see you around. Unless maybe you're leaving on safari tomorrow?"

"Been there. Done that."

He walked toward the door, shaking his head. "Where *haven't* you been, Abby Steel?"

Abby just smiled as a tidal wave of emotion threatened to break through her walls. He barely made it off the porch before she stopped him. "Wait. How did you know where I lived?"

He started walking backward, pulling his keys out of his pocket. "Jake."

That made sense. Fucking Jake was always shooting his mouth off. "I should have known."

He swung one leg over the Gold Wing. "See ya around?"

"Possibly."

Abby closed the door and pushed her back against it, just to make sure. She took a slow deep breath, trying to replace the oxygen that always seemed to get sucked out of her atmosphere when Trevor was around. It took a few moments to regain her center.

All at once he called her doubts and fears up to the surface, reducing her hard-won confidence to a shaky mass of uncertainty. *Coming home* was a concept that used to feel comforting. Now it felt awkward, and maybe even more dangerous than solo travel.

LATER, at Lauren's kitchen table, after the pictures were shared and the tales of adventure were told and the girls were blissfully enjoying their daily screen time in the adjacent room, she relayed the story of Trevor's visit.

The look on Lauren's face was priceless. "You're kidding me, right?"

"I couldn't make this shit up if I tried."

"What are you going to do?"

"Nothing. Why?"

"I don't know. It's just... I mean, it's Trevor."

She shoved Lauren hard in the arm. "It's ancient history, that's what it is."

"Apparently *not*." Lauren grabbed Abby's plate and started cleaning the table.

"What's that supposed to mean?"

Lauren stood there shaking her head and rubbing her arm as Jake walked in.

"What's wrong with your arm, babe?" He looked over. "Oh hey, Abby. Welcome back! You know I just saw Trev a couple days ago? He came in to talk about an old building off Silverado Trail."

Jake worked for one of the local banks handling commercial mortgages. What the hell would Trevor want with a commercial mortgage? Maybe his dad was looking to relocate the shop.

"Weird that you both came back at the same time, huh?"

"Even weirder that he just *happened* to know where I live." Abby glared at him.

"What?" Jake held up both hands. "He said he had something important to talk to you about. It's not like I gave him your phone number! Hell, I figured if he could catch you at home, he'd be doing better than ninety-nine percent of the rest of the planet, you know what I mean?" He grabbed an apple and took a big bite. "I thought I was doing you a favor."

"Yeah, well, next time, don't do me any *favors*. Got it?"

"Fine! Jesus. Welcome home, Miss Congeniality."

"All right, you two. Settle down." Lauren walked over and kissed Jake on the cheek. "How was your day?"

Jake didn't respond. He just stood there—across the room yet toe-to-toe with Abby. The silence went on for an uncomfortable amount of time.

Abby broke first. "I'm sorry, Jake. It's not your fault. It's just... he was the last person I expected to see at my door. I hadn't even been home twelve hours."

"Yeah, he kinda caught me off guard too."

Abby nodded.

"What was so important that he had to rush over there?" Jake asked.

Abby's eyes narrowed playfully. "Wouldn't you rather see pictures of an albino rhino?"

"Are you kidding?" He scoffed. "You and Trevor in the same room is *way* more interesting than an albino rhino."

There was truth on both sides of that statement. It was a curious anomaly, to be sure. It was also one of those rare things that would probably only be glimpsed once in a lifetime.

3

Abby was waiting for a piece of salmon to thaw as she finished up the last of her emails to the group going to Patagonia. Her next trip was coming up in two weeks, and life had been nonstop planning since she got back. After Argentina and Chile, she was doing back-to-back trips in other parts of South and Central America before returning to the States, so planning was in different stages for different groups.

The reviews on her website were consistently five stars, but the comments hardly ever had to do with the locations she picked and planned so meticulously. They would write one line about the beautiful scenery, and three or four about the deep, authentic relationships they formed within the group, frequently mentioning the *Question of the Day* cards Abby gave them.

The cards had been an evolution. It started with long conversations over extended mealtimes in the homes of new acquaintances she met along the way. Inevitably the questions they asked made her think more deeply about life, and about her reasons for traveling.

Later, after the meals were over, she would journal about

the questions she was asked, often discovering answers to the deep questions buried in her soul. If the questions had never been asked, Abby realized, she wouldn't have grown as much.

She kept track of the most important questions and wrote them down. As she grew more confident, she would turn these questions back on other people. Conversations turned from travel to philosophy, philosophy to politics, politics to religion. Wine was poured and discussions continued late into the evenings. She learned so much about the world and its people simply by paying attention, and in this way, acquaintances quickly became friends.

Abby started asking questions in her tour groups to break the ice and build relationships. She would share about her travel journals and the questions that changed the game for her, opening up discussions about life in the evenings over dinner. Rather than letting people eat and run, she encouraged them to linger, giving them a sense of what it was like in many different cultures worldwide.

It went really well. The women shared their struggles and gave one another support and advice, and once again, acquaintances quickly became friends. Eventually the questions became an important part of each day. She had them printed onto cards and the cards became a staple of the tours.

She did her best to get to know them as individuals and to make each trek meaningful for them—not because it was good for business, which it obviously was, but because she cared. These trips meant something to them. And to her as well. These relationships became her anchor in an ever-changing landscape. Staying connected gave her a purpose and kept her from drifting aimlessly around the globe.

Many of them wrote to her afterward with stories of how their lives had changed dramatically, and they credited their trip with Steel Journeys as the catalyst for those changes. They wrote about the questions they went home with—and how the answers were still forming in the tracks their adventures left behind. Word of mouth spread, and her tours were always full. It was humbling, to be sure.

So much time and effort had gone into building something she could be proud of, and her life was exactly where she wanted it to be. But she couldn't stop thinking about Trevor's visit. She hadn't heard from him again in the two weeks she'd been back, but his card, instead of being pitched when he walked out the door, had rather inconveniently found its way to the side of the fridge. Good thing Lauren hadn't been over or she'd never hear the end of it.

Still, a daughter? With Claire? It was so incredibly frustrating. That time in her life was something she tried hard to put behind her, but it wouldn't stay put. Abby rubbed the scar on her knee, and the memory flooded back just as clear as the night it happened.

CLAIRE HAD JUST BROKEN up with her boyfriend. She was a lot like Lauren—she always wanted to be a wife and a mother, but Justin got cold feet when she started talking about marriage. They were having a great time together, he said. Why did she have to go and ruin it by talking about forever? In Claire's mind, this meant he never loved her, which may have been true, but that only made it worse. She was a hot mess.

It was a warm summer night and there was supposed to be a meteor shower, which Trevor and Abby were planning to watch from a hayfield that bordered the local winery. Trevor worked at the winery so he knew the gate code, and they often went there to watch the stars. Abby couldn't stand the thought of leaving Claire alone, so they invited her along.

The pre-gaming started in the parking lot at Pop's Diner, but Abby had a headache, so she was the designated driver.

Trevor and Claire were already getting sloppy when they sat down for burgers, and by the time they settled the blankets in the field, Trevor's fifth of bourbon had been reduced by about half. He never was very good at fractions. It wasn't unusual for him to over-serve himself, and normally Abby was right there with him, but her head was absolutely pounding.

Trevor asked if she wanted him to go grab some Tylenol out of the winery office.

"There's no way you're getting behind the wheel, even if it *is* only a couple hundred yards across the parking lot. With our luck you'll run into the building and we'll lose our stargazing spot." She gave Trevor a knowing look. *Stargazing my ass.* They came out there to screw and they both knew it. "I can do it. I have to pee anyway."

"Are you sure?" he asked, slurring badly.

"I'll be right back." She kissed him, and he started to pull her down on top of him. "Slow down, cowboy. We've got company." She glanced over at Claire, who looked about ready to pass out.

Trevor's eyelids were all bunched up as he tried to focus on Claire. "Oh yeah!" he slurred again. "I forgot."

Abby waited with her arms crossed. Trevor had a weird quirk about holding onto the keys, even when he wasn't driving. He fished them out of his pocket with some difficulty and tossed them to her, falling over in the process. They'd probably both be out cold by the time she got back.

Abby knew the winery almost as well as he did. They'd had sex just about everywhere on that property, inside and out. She used the bathroom and found the Tylenol, as well as an unopened bag of potato chips in the break room.

She was watching the sky for meteors and munching on chips as she walked back through the field. Claire was making noises that sounded like half-laughing and half-crying. She didn't do breakups very well. She tended to be super emotional, and being drunk definitely didn't help, so Abby hurried along, wondering if her friend needed a shoulder to cry on.

Then she heard Trevor's ragged breathing through the darkness. Her mind couldn't reconcile the two sounds, so she switched on the flashlight. Nothing could have prepared her for seeing them both naked, with Trevor mounted on top of Claire. He collapsed onto her, blinking into the light as if it was an annoyance instead of a wake-up call.

"Who's there?" He put his hand up in front of his face, and rolled off Claire, wobbling badly, even though he was already horizontal.

Claire was squinting into the light as well. "Abby? Oh my God!" She grabbed the blanket and tried to cover herself, a useless but instinctive move.

Abby dropped the flashlight and chips and ran toward the truck. It was hard to see through the blur of tears and she tripped, landing hard on a rock and splitting her knee wide open. She kept on running until she reached the truck.

She left the two of them stranded in the field and peeled out of the parking lot, blood dripping down her leg onto the floorboard. Abby parked in front of Trevor's house, left the keys on the seat, and started to limp home, stopping from time to time, crying uncontrollably. When Lauren came to pick her up, they sat together on the side of the road. Lauren held her for a long time, letting her cry, but the bleeding wouldn't stop, so she took her to the hospital.

Nothing was broken, and eight stitches later, the doctor said her kneecap would heal with a scar, but there was nothing they could do about the fact that her heart was torn wide open. Everything she'd ever wanted was sitting back in that hayfield. A kind of numbness settled over the scene that night, a scab that formed a protective layer over the rush of emotions that had nowhere else to go. In time, the rest of her became numb enough to move on, but to do what? Her world had been built around Trevor and Claire.

Calistoga was a small town, and news traveled fast, so her mother arranged for her to spend the summer with her aunt up near Mt. Shasta. By the time she got back, Trevor and Claire had left town. That one explosion claimed everything she held dear. All that was left was a bunch of frayed relationships and a lot of loose ends. The problem with loose ends is that most people just stuff them under the rug. Or in this case, under the bed. God, he was good in bed...

THE SMELL of raw fish became harder to ignore, and the threads of memory loosened their grip on her. She tried to concentrate on emails and financials, but her kitchen felt small and stifling. It had been at least a year since her last decent lover, and before that it was a string of bad lays in multiple countries. Since the split with Eric, she rarely spent enough time in one place to get past meaningless sex—well, except for a steamy fling in Costa Rica last year with a white-water rafting guide named Alejandro.

Culture and language aside, sex proved to be a fairly level playing field. There were a few basic differences surrounding approach, of course, but execution had nothing to do with geography. That was all just personal style.

From what she remembered, Trevor was an incredible lover. Unfortunately, he was the measuring stick. She hated him for that, because apparently there weren't very many men like him. He was patient and kind, fiery and passionate, in constant waves that ebbed and flowed like the ocean. Their lovemaking had been epic and stretched for hours into the night.

She had loved him with all her heart, then hated him with her entire being.

Love and hate mingled together, and the memories of their physical connection tortured her until her panties were wet. She pushed back from the table. *This is ridiculous, Abby. Get ahold of yourself!*

S‍HE LEFT the fish on the counter, grabbed her keys and helmet, and fired up the Harley, taking every twisting back road until her head felt clear and her stomach required a meal. She knew the roads in and around the Coastal Mountains better than anywhere else in the world, and that was mostly thanks to Trevor. They were on his bike every spare minute, exploring the hills and valleys, vineyards and rivers that twisted their way through this fertile valley.

The day she climbed onto the back of his bike, the entire trajectory of her life changed. She tried to remember what she wanted to be or do before she met him, but nothing came to mind except journalism. She wrote for the school paper and liked traveling around and interviewing people to get their stories. She got a degree in psychology and minored in communications; neither area of study was in high demand in the general job market, but both served her well in the travel and tourism business.

Passing through the familiar downtown streets, she saw the quaint, early-twentieth-century architecture with new eyes. Buildings she had known since her youth had been taken over by sophisticated new restaurants, galleries, and boutiques. The town took full advantage of their presence at the northern tip of Napa Valley, where wine-country traffic and tourism now dictated much of the town's livelihood.

Abby too had built a business catering to people who wanted to travel and experience new places—a lesson she had learned from her entrepreneurial hometown. Now, when she traveled, she evaluated each town's amenities, cleanliness, and overall atmosphere as a potential tour stop, filtered through the lens of her business.

It was unsettling, this habit that had formed during her absence. Perhaps it was a function of maturity, the way a jungle gym looks so much smaller once you've grown too large to hang from the bars. Still, it was throwing her off-balance. She'd come back looking for a chance to regain her center, but now it seemed farther away than ever.

Calistoga was known for its spas and hot springs. Abby worked at one of the spas for a couple of years and used to love soaking in the hot springs after they closed to tourists. This was why she insisted on a condo with a soaking tub, and why she had visited every hot spring she could find along her tour routes ever since.

She passed the travel agency where she worked for a while. That was where she met Joe, one of the travel agents. He was a nice enough guy, and they dated for a few months, but he was too into the gym and fantasy football and just wasn't her type. Still, the knowledge and tools she gained working that job had really helped when it came to planning group tours and booking excursions. Funny how life sometimes leads you right down the path you're supposed to go. Looking back, it was as if the road that led to Steel Journeys had been paved ahead of time.

Then there was Eric. With him there had been real potential. They'd dated for almost two years. The sex was good, they liked the same movies, and he was a great cook. He moved from Phoenix to open a new restaurant in town. It was one of those trendy places where the kitchen was open and you could see all the chefs and sous chefs preparing meals in their white coats and hats. Abby absolutely adored his cioppino.

They met one day at the farmers' market. She was buying some fresh flowers for her mom's birthday when he walked by.

"Cioppino, right?"

"Excuse me?" She looked at him, confused. "Are you talking to me?"

"You always order the cioppino. I've seen you at my restaurant."

"Are you kidding?" Abby laughed. "I could eat my weight in that stuff! Are you the chef?"

"Guilty." He stuck out his hand. He had sandy brown hair, a clean-shaven face and a strong jaw. "I'm Eric."

"And I'm hungry, now that you've mentioned the cioppino. Get back in there and start cooking!" Abby pointed in the direction of the restaurant, which was only a couple of blocks away.

"Only if you'll come in tonight for dinner. I'll make you something special. What do you say?"

"Is there a downside to this deal?" Abby shook her head. "Of course I will."

"Great. The kitchen closes at nine. Why don't you come in about eight thirty? And come hungry!"

That night Eric wowed her with delicious food and wine, then they sat in the restaurant for a couple of hours critiquing the latest blockbusters and talking about motorcycles. He rode dirt bikes as a kid in Arizona but didn't have a street bike. Still, he liked that she rode and wasn't intimidated by the fact that she knew how to fix her own bike.

It felt good to laugh, and their personalities were well suited to one another. He liked his long hours and she liked her space. Being with him was healing, especially since he wasn't from Calistoga. Somehow it was easier, dating someone who didn't have her entire history in his back pocket.

Eric was good people. His restaurant partnered with the local food bank, reducing waste by donating their surplus, and the two of them cooked at the homeless shelter a couple of times a month. He even volunteered at the Red Cross for disaster relief. During the wildfires, when she was so far away, he was her lifeline, checking in on Lauren and Jake and keeping Abby posted as much as possible to set her mind at ease.

They probably would have moved in together if her parents hadn't died, but after that, something snapped inside, and all bets were off. She broke up with him and bought her own place, then decided to start the business and get out of Calistoga for a while. He still checked in from time to time, and they maintained an awkward sort of friendship.

She meant to call him, but then Trevor showed up and everything turned upside down.

She stretched her neck and turned her head at a stop sign, trying to work the tension out. A hot bath might be just the ticket, but first she needed to get something to eat. She missed his cioppino, but today was not that day.

Abby ended up at Pop's—a quintessential small-town diner at the far end of town. It had been there as long as she could remember. In fact, she learned to do her first figure eights in the diner's circular parking lot.

She parked her bike in the stretch out front that was reserved for motorcycles and draped her helmet over one of the handlebars. Pop's was a frequent stop for bikers. Besides, no one dared mess with any of the bikes parked out front. Pop was a reformed one-percenter. He never talked about which gang he belonged to, or that he'd done time earlier in his life, but when he got out of prison, he opened the diner and never looked back. He had his faults, but he was there for her when Trevor left town and had been an enormous support to Abby since her parents died.

As soon as she walked through the door, she heard Pop's gruff voice. "Well, what the devil have we got here? A ghost?"

Abby smiled and sat at one of the stools at the long counter. "Hey, Pop."

"Don't you *hey, Pop* me! Get your pretty little ass over here and give an old man a hug!"

Abby put aside her feminist tendencies where Pop was concerned. He threw these things out like terms of endearment, the way someone flips you off with a teasing smile. The words *politically correct* would just make him go off on a rant. She'd known Pop a long time, and his heart was pure gold. Besides, he didn't mean anything by it. He was just a crass old biker who loved fiercely and wasn't afraid to show it.

She hugged him and he held on tight, grabbing her shoulder muscles as he backed away as if to make sure she had all her parts put together correctly. "Where the hell have you been?"

She opened her mouth to speak but he cut her off and let go of her shoulders rather abruptly.

"Or should I say, where *haven't* you been?" He made his way back behind the counter.

"Have you been *stalking* me?" Abby tried to feign surprise.

He just grinned. Pop followed her travels on her website and social media, which, given his stance on most things technology, was a bit of a disconnect. Still, it was his seed money that gave her business its initial startup, even though she paid it back right after the inheritance came through. He was the one who pushed her out of the nest and told her to go follow her dreams, and he'd been her biggest fan and encourager since.

"I keep an eye on all my investments." He grabbed a cup and poured coffee she hadn't asked for.

"Is that all I am to you? An investment?" Abby pretended to stab her own heart and Pop's face broke into a huge grin.

Just then the door opened and Trevor walked in. He did a double take when he saw Abby.

"Jesus Christ, you too?" Pop blurted out. "What the hell is this, old home week?" He looked between the two of them, staring at each other. "Well, shit— I'm gonna go grill up a couple of burgers and a basket of fries."

"Abby!" Trevor looked almost embarrassed. He was dressed

in a pair of crisp-looking khakis and a button-down, with a copy of the *Wall Street Journal* under his arm.

She made no attempt to hide her surprise. "The *Journal*? Really?"

"I thought we weren't going to judge one another anymore."

Abby flushed. He was right. He just looked so different. It was hard to imagine him doing anything but wrenching on a bike and eating street tacos.

"What are you doing here?" He looked outside.

The Harley was clean again and shining in the afternoon sun. However, she didn't see the Gold Wing anywhere. "I just out clearing the cobwebs, you know?" She turned back toward the counter and picked up her coffee, suddenly thankful that Pop had poured it for her. "Where's your trusty steed?" she asked without turning around.

"At home. I brought my dad's truck because I have to pick Kelsey up after school. Do you mind if I sit down?"

"So polite," she mused, still staring straight ahead. When he slid onto the stool next to her, they were dangerously close again, and the clean smell of an understated cologne assaulted her senses. It didn't seem to matter that time had gone by. That rusty old switch may have been flipped off, but the electricity remained, pulsing through an invisible wire strung between them.

"Would you stop already? Can't we at least be friends?"

At least? "Friends. Hmmm. I'll have to think about that." She still refused to look at him. His hair was neatly tamed and the fresh shave was really throwing her. This was definitely not the Trevor she remembered.

He interrupted her thoughts just in time. "Actually, I have a favor to ask."

This ought to be good. "But I haven't given you an answer on the friendship thing. Are you even allowed to ask me a favor if we're not friends?"

He ignored the sarcasm and set his newspaper down. "This is more of a business proposition."

Abby pushed the coffee back and set her elbows on the counter. "Now this I've gotta hear." When she turned her head to look at him he didn't speak for a few seconds.

"What's the matter? Cat got your tongue?"

He took a deep breath. "Kelsey's looking for a part-time job."

"Maybe Pop's hiring." She opened her mouth to call out to the kitchen, but Trevor put his hand on her arm. The heat of his skin stopped her words and made her stiffen.

He inched his hand away. "I was wondering if she could work for you."

"For me?"

"She's a math nerd. A whiz at coding and graphic design."

"I'm not following."

"Well, I've been to your website, and you could use some help with branding."

"You've...been to my website?"

"Relax—it's not as creepy as it sounds."

"What a relief." Abby didn't know whether to be flattered that he'd looked up her website or offended that he thought it was a piece of shit.

"Listen, I just want to encourage her passions. Rather than have her get a job waitressing, I was hoping to find her some work in website development or design or something. I know she's young, but I'm telling you she's really good. Besides, a job like that won't necessarily take her away from her schoolwork for hours at a time. She's still fragile. Staying with my parents has given her a safe place to land, but I'd like to keep her close to home for a while yet."

Abby tried to listen but his words kept spinning in circles in her mind.

"You wouldn't have to pay her much. I'd just like her to get some experience. And if you hate her designs, you don't have to use them."

"Why not have her work for your dad? Surely his image needs an update."

"It does. But that's not the point."

"Then what *is* the point?"

"I told you—I'm trying to do the right thing."

"So why can't you leave me out of it?" Her frustration was rising.

He didn't say anything. He just let her come at him.

Why couldn't he see the uncomfortable position he was putting her in? "Listen, Trev, it's not that I'm opposed to redoing the site, but I don't think you understand what you're asking." She kept shaking her head, trying to get her point across.

He grabbed her hand. She tried to pull away but he held tight. "I do. I get it. But we're here trying to make a fresh start, and I want her to be around strong women. Women who have been through hard times but carried on. Women who mentor other women."

He had obviously done his homework and read the reviews. It was a calculated move. She wanted to toss the rest of her coffee in his face. "Are you fucking kidding me right now?"

"What you've built is amazing. I want her to see that she can aspire to something great."

Abby's pulse was rising. She had no idea how to frame this in her head, much less her heart. She ripped her hand out of his grasp. "Let's recap, shall we? Less than two weeks ago, you showed up at my door to tell me that all those years ago you had a love child with my best friend—a decision that categorically ruined our plans for a life together."

There was no sense beating around the bush. She might as well speak the truth and lay it out there, but when Pop looked up from behind the counter, she tried to lower her voice.

"Now that her mother is dead, you want *me* to take her under my wing and mentor her?"

"It sounds a lot worse when you say it that way."

"Which way? When I tell the truth? Maybe if you'd told the truth fifteen years ago, things would be different! What you're asking is too much."

"It's only too much if you still care about me, but you've made it pretty clear that you don't," he shot back. "Something along the lines of *that ship sailed a long time ago.* This is a business proposition, Abby. From what I can tell, you spend so much time on the road, you don't have a lot of time for social media and website building. This is win-win. It would give Kelsey some real-world experience and something to put in a design portfolio, and it would give you a better chance at expanding your business. This has nothing to do with you and me."

She sat there staring at him, her chest heaving with anger at the blatant disregard for her feelings. "I'm leaving for Patagonia in another couple weeks. After that I'll be in Brazil and then Costa Rica. It'll be nearly spring before I get back here."

"God, I'm jealous." He shook his head. "I sure hope you take a lot of pictures."

"I do. Not that I have time to organize or categorize them. Stop changing the subject."

"I'm not. I'm making a point. Perhaps a virtual assistant is just what the doctor ordered." He flipped his palm in the air as if it was already a done deal. "You could upload pictures and she could post them to social media for you. This is the digital age, Abby. As long as you have a laptop you can connect from anywhere in the world. Just meet with her once, that's all I'm asking. Give the kid a shot."

"Jesus, Trev. You're breaking my heart." Abby didn't even try to hide the sarcasm. She just looked straight ahead.

"I just moved her to a brand-new state and a brand-new school. She needs something positive to focus on right now."

Abby was fuming at his presumption. Just then Pop set baskets of burgers and fries in front of them.

"Thanks, Pop." Trev smiled at him, but Pop was watching for Abby's reaction.

"I think one of you needs to go sit in another part of the restaurant."

"You know what?" Abby pushed up from the stool. "I need to go anyway. Trevor can have my burger. He looks like he could use a few more pounds. It was good to see you, Pop. I'll come back another time."

"Abby, wait!"

Trev started to go after her, but Pop grabbed his shoulder. "Leave it."

Trevor huffed out a breath.

Pop laughed. "Well, it's good to know some things never change. You two always were like fire and ice."

Abby pulled open the door and didn't look back. It wasn't hard to tell which one of them was ice.

4

———

The road called her back up into the hills, and it was nearly dark before Abby got home. Three hours of winding curves were spent trying to straighten out the thoughts that raged within her. As she parked the bike back in front of her condo and hit the kill switch, she wished she could shut down the whole conversation. Unfortunately, when she got inside and opened her email, there was a new message in her inbox. The subject line read: *Ideas for your new website.*

It was from Kelsey. Trevor hadn't wasted any time.

The fish was still on the counter, so she prepped it quickly and tossed it in the oven with a few vegetables and opened a bottle of wine. She sat in the kitchen with her laptop, answering a few other emails, and getting a little of the wine in her veins before clicking back to the message from Kelsey. Abby was pissed, but it was hard to blame the girl. Trevor was the one pushing this agenda, and there was no telling what he might have said to her.

There was a video embedded in the email. The thumbnail showed a smiling blonde teenager seated in front of a computer. She looked a lot like Trevor and very little like Claire.

It was hard to look at her face without remembering the scene from that night. She imagined their first meeting. *Hi Kelsey, I'm Abby. I used to be friends with your mom. In fact, funny story—I was actually <u>there</u> when you were conceived.*

Abby wondered once again how Trevor could possibly have known she would be at the diner. Indeed, the look of surprise when he saw her seemed genuine enough. She sighed audibly and pressed play. She might as well listen to what the girl had to say.

Hi, Abby. My name is Kelsey. My dad said you might be open to some help with your website. Before you turn this video off, just hear me out. I started learning coding and website development three years ago when I started middle school. I got put in some advanced classes for girls who were interested in web design. It was a pilot program funded by some companies that wanted to encourage young girls to go after careers in technology. I also took a college-level course in graphic design and mixed media last summer. And let's face it, I'm fifteen and I think I've got the whole social media thing figured out.

Kelsey giggled a little, and when she smiled one of her eyes crinkled just like Trevor's. Abby swallowed and kept watching.

I want to show you a mock-up of an idea I had.

Suddenly the screen cut to a compilation of some of the images from Abby's website as well as videos of women riding difficult trails in beautiful locations all superimposed over a whole new design. Images flashed in and out as she set the fresh, dynamic website side by side with her current website design, which was basic and functional but boring by comparison.

Kelsey's voiceover explained, *Obviously I would need time to personalize all the pictures and talk with you about what you want. I could help you with Instagram and Facebook too. I just want to say that I think your company is super cool and I love the idea of women leading women around the globe. I was thinking that could be worked into the tagline for the website.*

38

Also, I came up with three new logo ideas, and if you like any of them let me know and we can change them to fit your needs.

One of the three designs caught Abby by the throat. It was a simple rendition of a woman on a bike next to a twisting road, with mountains on one side and an ocean on the other. In the drawing the woman's arms were stretched out above her head. Abby paused the video.

Somehow this girl had captured her essence in one fell swoop. That was impossible. There was no way she could have known or even intuited that this was an actual event. Trevor must have had a hand in this.

No one else would have known about that trip. But Trevor wasn't even the keeper of that photograph, was he? It was taken on one of those disposable cameras they used to bring on their road trips and develop the pictures when they got home. Back before every cell phone had a camera and sharing memories was as easy as the click of a button. Trevor never kept paper photographs. He said it made him sad when they yellowed and faded and putting them in fancy albums was a waste of time and money.

She went to her closet and pulled a box off the top shelf, rifling through ticket stubs and weird souvenirs until she found it. She brought the photo back to the kitchen and compared it to Kelsey's design. It was nearly exact. Impossible.

The timer dinged for the fish, so she turned the oven off and pulled it out, picking at the food right out of the casserole dish. By the time she finished half her dinner and another glass of wine, the suspense was killing her.

She pulled Trevor's card off the fridge and dialed the number. It went to a very professional-sounding voicemail with Trevor's smooth voice promising to return the call the next business day. At this point, Abby was pacing the kitchen with her wine glass in one hand and her phone in the other.

"What the hell are you trying to prove, Trevor? You show up

39

here and assume everything can just pick up where it left off? It was half a lifetime ago and yet...by the way, how did you get a copy of that picture? Did you keep the negatives?" She stopped talking long enough to take another sip of wine. "The irritating part is that I like her ideas. I'm not saying I'm going to hire her. There are just so many questions without answers here and... Oh, fuck it! You suck, ok? I just called to tell you that you suck."

She started to hang up then pulled the phone back to her ear. "Oh, and by the way, this is Abby."

She sat down hard in a kitchen chair, frustrated with her lack of self-control. "Well, *that* was a stupid move," she said out loud.

She left the food on the counter and took a hot bath, trying to relax the tension in her shoulders that had been there all day. She pulled on an oversized sleep shirt and decided to let her hair air-dry. Maybe some brainless movie would take her mind off things. The wine was over half-gone when she set the bottle on the coffee table and switched on the TV. The doorbell rang, and she looked at the clock. It was only seven thirty but still, a little late for solicitors.

Rather than put on some pants she opened the door just a crack to tell whoever it was to fuck off, but it was Trevor. Again. The words nearly slipped out of her mouth anyway. Unfortunately, this time it wasn't his fault. She was the one who made the ranting phone call.

"*Now* what?"

He smiled and shook his head. "It's nice to see you again too."

"Déjà vu. What can I do for you, Trev?"

"I got your voicemail."

She could feel color creeping into her face. "Yeah. Sorry about that."

She started to close the door on him, but he stuck his hand

out. "I wanted a chance to explain myself. Will you at least give me that?"

The wine was making her head fuzzy. It seemed like a good idea, which must mean it was a terrible idea. She shook her head to clear it.

"So that's a no, then?"

"What? No. I mean, ok."

"How much have you had to drink?" He smiled and his eyes were laughing at her. Or maybe she was hallucinating. He still hadn't moved off the porch.

She wasn't sure if he was trying to be cocky or charming, but it was annoying as fuck. She had questions and she wanted answers, damn it, so she stood there debating. The fact that she was leaving again soon was not lost on her. Leaving behind so many unknowns might drive her insane. She pulled open the door. As he stepped through it, he handed her a bottle of wine, then looked down at her bare legs sticking out of the bottom of her T-shirt.

"What's this?" she asked.

"Peace offering."

"Well, I've already got one open, but thanks. You can put it in the kitchen." She handed it back to him. "I'm going to go put some pants on."

"You don't have to do that on my account." Trevor's eyes twinkled.

"You haven't changed a bit." She rolled her eyes and headed toward the bedroom. She could feel him watching her, so she turned around to walk backward. Sure enough, he was still standing in the same spot, staring at her. "There some salmon in there if you're hungry, unless of course those two burgers filled you up at lunch."

Abby went to the bedroom and pulled on some yoga pants. She probably needed to put a bra on too. Her body had no secrets from Trevor, but tempting fate was never a good idea where that man was concerned.

It wasn't like she was in there long, but when she came out, he was sitting on her couch with a plate of food and a glass of wine.

"Comfy?" His presumption was astounding.

"I wasn't going to eat, but I took a bite of the salmon and it was really good! What'd you put on top?"

She picked up her glass and sat on the opposite end of the couch. Intentionally. The gesture wasn't lost on him and he laughed softly.

"It's a mixture of butter, soy, lemon, and brown sugar." It was Eric's concoction, something easy she'd picked up from him making special meals for homeless people.

"It's fantastic!" He forked some into his mouth with enthusiasm. His mother was a fantastic cook, and he always appreciated a good meal.

Abby sipped her wine, watching him eat. She tried to think about all the questions that were in her mind earlier, but there was only one that really caused a splinter. She went to the kitchen and retrieved the photograph, the one Trevor had taken of her on Highway 1 somewhere south of Santa Cruz.

She dropped it on the table next to him. "How?"

He looked down at the photograph. He looked up at her. Slowly he swallowed his food. "It's stuck. In my mind. It's how I always think of you."

"But—"

"No, I didn't keep the negatives." He pointed to his temple. "It's just in here."

Abby tried to digest that comment. Tried to acknowledge the implications of what it could mean. "I don't understand."

Trevor put his plate down. "Listen, I took two pictures that day. One on the camera and one in my mind. The one in my mind is as clear and detailed as the one here—maybe more so.

I can still remember how it smelled, and what the air felt like. The food we ate that morning." He looked down at his shoes. "And the love we made that night."

Abby remembered it, too. They slept on the beach in one of those pop-up shelters that looked like a clam shell, making a bed out of two large travel blankets and the rest of their gear. They built a fire for the first part of the night and kept each other warm for the second. Sleep came in two- or three-hour increments in those days, in between lovemaking sessions that made them lose track of time.

That night had been special. Trevor spent hours appreciating every inch of her body by the light of a full moon. It was the first night they professed their love for one another. Abby had just turned twenty-one.

Both stubborn by nature, they'd spent months traveling and exploring together. Making love but never actually talking about love. Something about that big full moon changed everything, though. His voice was soft, his touch gentle, and everything seemed framed in light. That was the night that she knew, beyond a shadow of a doubt, that she wanted to spend the rest of her life with him, no matter where the road might lead.

"When Kelsey looked at your website, she asked me to tell her about you. She wanted to know what was unique about you, so she could design a logo."

"And that's the memory you picked?"

"Yes," he said without apology. "I told her you were always trying to find the road to freedom. That it had taken you just about everywhere. But that you found a taste of it right there, between the mountains and the sea. That was the happiest I'd ever seen you."

"So she knows about us."

"Yes."

"What did you tell her?"

"That you were my first love."

Abby looked down. He didn't elaborate, but then again, he didn't have to. In that moment it didn't matter that they'd spent fifteen years apart. It didn't matter that Trevor had been with someone else all those years, even if it was *on and off* as he described it. Miles of history stretched between them. And truth. Undeniable truth.

The silence was filled with everything but words. He poured them both another glass of wine and disposed of the empty bottle. When he came back from the kitchen, he was carrying the other bottle in one hand. His other was up in the air, to stop the words from coming out of her mouth.

"Before you say anything, I'm not that guy anymore. I don't drink the brown stuff. It's beer or wine only, and I know how to keep myself in check. Helps me keep my girlish figure." He winked.

She couldn't help but smile, shaking her head. "Your figure is anything but girlish." Somewhere between his twenties and thirties he'd developed a broad chest and a decent set of biceps. She could feel the familiar pangs of want rising up, unbidden.

His gaze trailed her shirt, stopping at her chest. She watched his eyes flicker before he looked away. When she glanced down, her nipples were standing up beneath the apparently too-thin bra she'd chosen. She couldn't help her reaction to him. It had been that way for as long as she'd known him, even before they started dating.

They spent hours together at his parents' house, working on motorcycles together in a hot garage, and yet her tank top would always betray her. He used to tease her relentlessly about how excited she got wrenching on bikes and how her *enthusiasm* was a *real turn-on*.

She tried to shove the memories out of her mind. "That picture was taken a long time ago, Trevor. A lot of things have changed since then."

"Yes, a lot of things have, but *you* haven't." He sat, pointing to the photo. "Inside, you're still this girl. And that's why Kelsey's design fits so well. Look." He pointed again. "It's got the element of freedom built right into the design. The mountains and the ocean represent world travel over all sorts of terrain, and the woman on the bike is saying, 'You can do this! You can have it all, and I'm going to show you how to get it.' There's a reason this day is stuck in my mind. And there's a reason it's in yours, too. It was the first time you started to believe in yourself. To believe in love."

"Yeah, well, look how well that turned out." She downed the last of her wine, putting her fingers to her forehead to stay the inevitable rush.

"Slow down, cowgirl." He reached for her glass and set it on the table. He took one of her hands and moved closer to her on the couch. "Listen, I didn't know you'd be at Pop's today, and I promise I'm not stalking you. I told her not to send the email until I'd talked to you about it, and when I told her I saw you today, she got all excited. I said you were thinking about it. That's all, I swear."

Abby pulled her hand away. "But that logo—that didn't just come up this afternoon."

"No." He looked at the floor. "It didn't."

"Why do I get the sense that I'm not going to like the rest of this story?"

"A couple of weeks after Claire died, Kelsey got a wild idea. The psychologist said it was normal. Anyway, she started talking about how you only live once, you know? She decided she wanted to learn to ride."

"So? Teach her. You get to call the shots now. You're the surviving parent." For some reason the words *surviving parent* triggered a sadness she was unprepared for.

"She asked me if I knew any women who rode, so I told her about you. We looked you up online and found an article in the local paper about your company. That's when we went to your website." Trevor looked at the table instead of her face.

"And?"

"She became kind of obsessed with the idea of women and motorcycles. She started doing research all on her own. Your story intrigues her. She wants to travel the world. She wants to see it all before she gets diagnosed with some terminal disease. Listen, I know it's not exactly a healthy coping mechanism, but it hasn't been that long since she lost her mom. She's just trying to cope."

Abby understood on a visceral level what it meant to lose a parent. It created a sort of identity crisis that took time to reconcile. Especially if Kelsey and Claire had been close, and Abby couldn't imagine Claire having a daughter that she wasn't close with, especially if she was mostly a single parent. What exactly did *on and off* look like?

"Claire used to cut hair for the woman who gave Kelsey piano lessons, kind of a barter system. So one day she asked if I thought you might be willing to teach her how to ride if she did some design work for you. At the time, we had just decided to move here and I didn't even know if you lived around here anymore."

"I'm not a replacement for her mother. If anything, I'm the antithesis of Claire. Not to mention she would be rebelling against the fact that her mom forbade her to ride."

"Claire didn't want her to ride because she always felt threatened by you, and because she felt so guilty for tearing us apart."

Abby sat up. "That is not my problem. None of this is my problem, and I can't believe you're playing the dead mom card on me."

Trevor sighed. "I don't blame you for being mad. For a whole lifetime of anger, ok? I'm just trying to help Kelsey through this transition. I don't know what I'm doing, Abbs. I missed the last several years of her life almost completely. When Claire got sick, I was in school in another state."

"You were where?"

"It's a long story. The point is, I'm still getting to know Kelsey. The psychologist said she needs stability. Something positive to focus on. So here we are, back with family. And here I am, asking you to give her something positive to focus on. This isn't about you and me. It's about Kelsey. And I don't know anyone who's stronger or more accomplished than you."

It was tremendously unfair of him to ask these things, but she felt trapped by Kelsey's admiration paired with their shared experience of loss. "Am I supposed to believe that I'm the only woman you know who rides? You can't tell me you've been celibate all this time."

His head popped back in surprise. "What does sex have to do with riding?"

"You tell me," she answered with a sneer. "It always seemed to be a trigger for you."

"No, Abby. *You* were the trigger."

His comment stopped her heart momentarily. She swallowed with some difficulty as he let the words hang in the air. It didn't make any sense.

"I thought Jim Beam was the trigger."

"Oh, now that hurts."

"If the shoe fits."

He let her words hang in the air for a moment before he spoke. "If anything I hated the drinking as much as you did, because I lost some of the sensation I came to crave."

His candor was startling, his words matter-of-fact. Abby was silent for a long time, but when she finally spoke, her shoulders had relaxed, and she leaned back into the couch cushions. "She looks just like you, you know."

He smiled. "Yeah, I know. Poor kid."

5

The next day, Abby sent Kelsey a response, asking if she wanted to be her virtual assistant on a three-month trial. Kelsey's response included an abundance of exclamation points. She even requested a meeting to go over the details.

Abby suggested a local coffee shop with decent Wi-Fi, but Kelsey wanted to meet at Pop's. There was no end to the irony. She tried not to think about that night, mostly because it felt like picking at a scab. For some reason, being at Pop's in general wasn't a trigger. Meeting Kelsey for the first time at Pop's was something different altogether.

On the day of their meeting, Abby was strangely nervous. She washed and waxed her bike until it shined and picked several different outfits before settling on jeans and a simple red sweater with her riding boots. She pulled her hair loosely into a ponytail at the back of her neck and even put on makeup, which for her involved little more than a light application of mascara, some cream blush, and a bit of tinted lip gloss. *Well, here goes nothing.* With her laptop and briefcase in the saddle bags, she stalled as long as she could until there was nothing left to do but ride over there.

The road opened out before her and began to calm her nerves, as it always did, but she couldn't stop thinking about Claire, their former friendship, and slumber party promises that one day their children would play together. Things didn't always work out the way they were supposed to.

She and Claire had both swooned over Trevor when he'd moved to town and enrolled in school halfway through senior year. He was the epitome of a bad boy with a motorcycle to boot. It was hard for any of the girls to resist that smile, and she supposed Claire just melted underneath him like the rest of them.

The image of Claire under him made her blood boil all over again and she turned down a back road, pulled the throttle, and attacked the road until it was out of her system. It wasn't all Claire. It took two to...well, it took both of them, anyway.

Thanks to a V-Twin engine and a little anger, even with the back roads detour, she pulled into the parking lot at Pop's right on time. It didn't occur to Abby that Trevor might be driving Kelsey to the diner until it was too late. She parked the bike and there he was, leaning against his dad's old pickup truck with his arms folded, a pretty blonde teenager standing right beside him. It was the same truck Abby had driven from the hayfield that night, and she briefly wondered if her blood was still stuck somewhere between the floorboards.

The way he watched her dismount and shake her hair out of the helmet made her warm in all the wrong places. She stowed her helmet and walked over to them, trying her best to ignore Trevor and focusing instead on the girl she was here to see.

Kelsey was literally in between them. The visual was a sobering reminder that none of this was the girl's fault. Abby's beef was with Trevor and with Claire, and Kelsey was an innocent by-product of their mistakes.

"You must be Kelsey!" Abby tried to sound excited. She took the girl's hand. "It's so good to meet you!"

"You too." Kelsey smiled. "I feel like I know all about you." Abby glanced at Trevor, who suddenly found a new scratch on his dad's old truck.

"I was so sorry to hear about your mother," Abby said, as sincerely as she could. "She and I were good friends, back in the day." That much at least was true, and Kelsey didn't need to be burdened with the rest. Her memories of her mother needed to remain intact.

Kelsey held on longer than was comfortable, looking at Abby's nails. "You have hands like hers."

Abby wondered how many hours Kelsey spent at her mother's bedside at the end of her life. She flashed back to a memory from childhood. She and Claire had their hands pressed against each other, marveling at the fact that they were exactly the same size. Even as they both moved awkwardly through puberty, they ended up being a similar height, sharing the same clothes. Even their feet were the same size.

Abby pulled her hand away and led Kelsey inside, looking over her shoulder. "You don't have to stay if you don't want to. I brought an extra helmet. I can run her home." She winked at Trevor and he smiled.

Kelsey's face lit up with anticipation. "Can I, Dad? Can I take ride on Abby's motorcycle?"

"Um. Yeah, I guess so." Trevor stuffed his hands in his pockets. Making fatherly decisions about a young girl's safety was clearly not in his wheelhouse. Abby felt a twinge of remorse for her earlier anger. For all his faults, he probably *was* doing the best he could.

She turned her attention back to Kelsey. "Tell me you've had one of Pop's famous milkshakes!"

"No, but my dad says they're great! That's why I wanted to come here."

Even after they went inside, Trevor stood by the truck watching them. Kelsey's back was to the window, but Abby could see him just fine. It was hard to say which of the two things was making her more uncomfortable: knowing he was watching her, or sitting across from the child he had with Claire.

She tried to ignore him but realized her laptop was still on the bike. Pop came over to say hello to Kelsey, giving Abby the chance to excuse herself.

"Hey, can you hang out here for a minute? I need to grab something off my bike."

He looked out the window at Trevor, then back at Abby. "Sure thing, honey."

"Thanks. I'll have my usual."

Trevor hadn't moved. He was still watching her as she retrieved the briefcase from her saddle bags.

"Are you going to stand there the whole time?" she wondered aloud.

"I haven't decided yet. I'm a little jealous, you see."

"Jealous? Of what? You want a milkshake too?"

"That Kelsey gets to ride with you and I don't. What do you say we take the Old Mountain Road Saturday afternoon? Weather's supposed to be perfect."

"Are you asking me on a date?"

"Nope." He grinned. "Just want to go riding with an old friend."

"Who are you calling old?"

"What do you say, Abby? For old times' sake?"

"There's that *old* word again." Her grip tightened around the briefcase. Small talk was not her forte. "You sure you can keep up with me on that big old bagger of yours?"

"There's that old word again."

Abby laughed. "Touché."

"Don't you worry about me. If memory serves, I'm pretty sure I can handle myself where you're concerned."

"Is that right?"

"Yeah. That's right."

She closed and relocked the bags then turned to face him. "You know, they say memory is the first thing to go. Your pride might be next."

THE MEETING with Kelsey went surprisingly well. Abby genuinely liked her ideas, and the kid really was a whiz with social media. Right there in the diner, she took the laptop and put all of Abby's travel pictures on a shared drive that would upload automatically from Abby's phone. This way, when she was traveling, Kelsey could pull pictures from various adventures and post something online a couple times a week.

Abby said no to the automatic upload idea and agreed instead to update the shared folder manually. She explained that often her pictures had nothing to do with the travel and this way they wouldn't get all mixed up. In reality she wanted to spare the poor girl any inadvertent disclosures from those occasional not-so-lonely nights on the road. However, she did agree to let Kelsey have a go at redesigning the website.

Passwords, logins, and phone numbers were exchanged, and they decided to meet one more time before she left for South America. Abby agreed to pay her two hundred dollars a month to be her virtual assistant. Kelsey was beyond excited.

"Let's start right away! I want to take a couple of pictures outside the diner with you next to your bike. It's super shiny, and you look really pretty today."

"I do?" Abby blinked.

"Yeah. I think my dad noticed too." Kelsey smiled.

"Kelsey, I—"

"It's ok. He told me you guys were in love once. He and my mom were never in love, but he tried real hard."

Abby sighed. She needed to change the subject. "Pictures, huh? Of me?"

"Yes, now come on!" Kelsey pulled her out of her seat.

"Hey, Pop? Do you mind if some pictures of your diner end up on the internet?" Abby called out as she was dragged toward the door. Although most restaurants and businesses loved the free publicity, she'd learned to ask permission.

He just waved them out without looking. "Whatever you need, darlin'!"

After Kelsey posed her several times and took pictures from different angles with her phone, Abby stowed all their gear and pulled the extra helmet out of her bag.

"You ready?"

Kelsey's eyes got wide and she nodded enthusiastically.

"You've really never been on a bike before? That's hard to believe, knowing your father."

She shook her head. "My mom would never let me. Dad always had to park his bike and take her car whenever we went anywhere together."

"Then you're in for a treat." She helped Kelsey adjust the helmet properly and explained what it meant to be on the back of a bike, where to put her feet and how to lean with the turns.

"This is a lot smaller than my dad's bike."

"It's a hybrid."

"You mean it runs on both gas and electricity?"

"No, silly." She tucked a stray piece of Kelsey's hair into the helmet. "It means it's lighter and more agile than a bagger, but it still has a big, powerful engine, so you can take it long distances."

"What's a bagger?"

"It's a nickname for bikes like your dad's that have all the creature comforts like cruise control, a built-in sound system, and navigation. He has that big windshield and a faring for wind protection in the front, and all the storage bags in the back."

"So, does your bike go faster than his?"

"Depends on who you ask."

She got them all situated and edged out onto the road with Kelsey tucked in behind her. When she pulled the throttle the first time, Kelsey squealed with delight and held on even tighter.

Abby took them down a couple of back roads with easy turns that wound around a section of woods where the sunlight was dappling through the trees.

"Oh my gosh! This is so amazing!" Kelsey screamed into Abby's ear.

"I can hear you just fine," Abby called back in a semi-normal voice.

"Oh! Sorry!" Kelsey yelled again. "It's just so beautiful!"

The rest of the ride all Abby heard was *wow* and *woo-hoo!* When they pulled into the driveway at Trevor's parents' house, Kelsey literally jumped off the bike and screamed the word "Yes!"

She unbuckled her helmet and pulled it off, spiking it down on the driveway like a football player in the end zone. "That was the most incredible thing I've ever done! Will you *please* teach me to ride?"

Abby blinked a couple of times, looking between the helmet and the girl with the enormous smile. "Um... When do you turn sixteen?"

"In three months."

"Ok, well, in California you have to be fifteen and a half to get a permit, but you also have to take drivers ed and a training course. Either that or wait until you're seventeen and a half if you don't want to take the classes."

"How much are the classes?"

"I don't know. I haven't looked into it in a long time."

"Well, with my new part-time job, maybe I can save up."

"Sounds like a great goal. Once you get your permit, I'd be happy to teach you how to ride, but I'm afraid that from now on, you can't ride with me anymore."

"Why not?"

Abby got off the bike and walked over to the helmet Kelsey had been wearing. "Here's your first lesson: A helmet is only engineered for one good fall—whether it's on or off your head. You protect your helmet at all times because as soon as it drops on the ground, you can no longer guarantee it will protect your head."

"But it doesn't look broken. It looks fine."

"On the outside it looks fine, yes. But we can't tell by looking at it if the inner shell is broken or compromised, so we can't ever use this one again. We don't take chances with our brains. Ever." Abby made a point of opening Gil's garbage can and tossing it in. "You can break almost every bone in your body and still recover, but if you break your head, you'll never be the same. Can you remember that?"

Kelsey nodded. "Oh my gosh, Abby! I'm so sorry!"

"I'm just glad your head wasn't in it when it hit the ground."

"I'll buy you a new one, I promise."

"Don't worry about it. Lesson learned, yes?" Kelsey kept nodding but her eyes filled with tears. Abby walked over and put an arm around her shoulders. "Hey now, it's ok. No need to cry. Was I too hard on you?"

Kelsey shook her head.

"Then what is it?"

"What if I want to go for another ride?"

Abby burst out laughing and gave her shoulders a squeeze. "You're definitely your father's daughter! I guess we'll just have to get you a new one, won't we?"

Just then, Trevor's dad swung open the front door and

walked over to where they were standing. "Would you look what the cat dragged in!"

"Hi, Grandpa." Kelsey smiled, wiping her tears.

"Now what's this about?" He dried her eyes the rest of the way with his thumbs.

"Oh, you know—" Abby interjected before Kelsey could rat herself out. "The visor was up on the ride and the wind made her eyes water."

"That'll teach you."

Abby smiled. "I'm pretty sure Kelsey learned her lesson."

"I think your grandma has supper ready," Gil announced.

"Whoops." Kelsey looked down at her shoes. "I just had a burger and a milkshake."

"I'm sure it'll keep a while. Why don't you run in and see?"

"Ok. Thanks for everything, Abby! I won't let you down!" She gave Abby an awkward hug and ran in the house.

Kelsey's exuberance was infectious. "It's good to see you, Gil." Abby reached for the older man's hands and he pulled her into an embrace instead.

"Well, if you aren't a sight for sore eyes! How've you been?" He held her at arm's length the same way Pop had, looking, it seemed, for any loose or wobbly parts. "I hear all kinds of crazy stories about your escapades!"

"No broken bones, I promise. And don't worry—only *half* of the crazy ones are true." She winked.

Still he wouldn't let go of her shoulders. "You are just as pretty as the day Trevor brought you home."

Abby shifted uncomfortably. Gil always said exactly what was on his mind. She used to stay up late talking to him, after Trevor had passed out for the night. At one point, he even told her she should break up with him until he got his act together. In many ways Trevor's parents and sister had been like her own family, and she'd missed them.

"Thanks, Gil, but you don't have to be so nice. It's not like I came around to see you after everything went south."

"And who could blame you? That knucklehead son of mine messed up the only good thing he ever had. Not that we aren't in love with that little Kelsey. She's cute as a button and smart as a whip."

"That she is."

"You know, took him a little too long to figure things out, but Trevor's done real good for himself. And looking after his responsibilities like this...well, we're just real proud of him. And you too! You always were our favorite."

"Good to know. Well, Gil, it's been nice—"

"You know you're the only girl he *ever* brought around."

Abby sighed internally. "I find that hard to believe, Gil. As I recall, he was quite the ladies' man when we were younger. I think you're just trying to make me feel better."

"Not one. Ever," Gil stated, holding up his fingers. "Scout's honor."

"Well, I can assure you all the girls liked him. Anyway, it's ancient history now. I'm so glad you and Renee—"

"You were his whole world." Gil looked at her as if to say *didn't you know?*

She was trying to exit the conversation gracefully, but Gil wasn't making it easy. What on earth was he rambling about? Gil was from Tennessee, and he could ramble with the best of them.

"We never even met Claire. She went off and moved across the country, and he went over there a couple times, but it never did fit right and then he just...drifted. Odd jobs, a couple different failed business ideas."

"I'm so glad he's turned things around. Even got his MBA!"

"Yup. Yup. He's done real good."

"I hear he's going to help you out around the shop."

"He's been threatening for years now to *revitalize* my business. I keep telling him I'm too old to be re-vit-a-lized. I told him if he wants to, he can come run it. So he finally took me up on my offer."

When Gil smiled, she could see how proud he was. "I'm so glad to hear that. Sounds like you two have a good working relationship. Listen, Gil, I have to run, but please give my love to Renee."

"All right now, don't you be a stranger, ok? We'd love to have you to supper one of these nights."

"Well, I'm leaving next week for Central and South America for a few months. Maybe when I get back?"

"How about Sunday? Renee's making her pot roast!"

"Tempting." Abby put her hand on her belly for effect. "But I have a lot to do getting prepared for my trip."

"Well, you know Renee. There'll be enough to feed the whole neighborhood, so just stop by if you can!"

She put on her best Southern accent and tipped her invisible cowboy hat. "Thanks, Gil. That's mighty kind of you."

Gil just smirked. "You city girls are all the same." He looked hurt as Abby started for her bike. "What, no hug for old Gil?"

"But you just hugged me three minutes ago!" she teased.

He pulled her into another embrace and whispered in her ear, "I mean it now. Don't be a stranger."

He kissed her on the cheek, and her heart melted a little. She missed her own dad like crazy, and Gil was such a kind and gentle soul. Trevor had been just like him once. Maybe he still was, not that she'd given him much of a chance.

Her heart softened momentarily, but on the ride home, she reminded herself of all the reasons he didn't deserve a chance. Betrayal was the kind of cut that went deep enough to leave a nasty scar, and this one had disfigured their relationship beyond recognition. It was permanent, and poor Kelsey was living proof of their reality.

~

LAUREN just about shit her pants when Abby called and told her everything.

"Jesus, Abby, you've been home for two weeks and you've got more drama than a romance novel—without the hot sex scenes."

"It's not drama! It's just loose ends."

"Unless—*did* you leave out any hot sex scenes?"

"No! Of course not."

"Of course not?" Skepticism dripped from Lauren's voice. "You do know who you're talking to, right? I learned everything I knew about sex from my *Tales with Trevor* bedtime stories."

"You were seventeen! You make it sound like I corrupted your morals."

"No. Jake corrupted my morals," Lauren answered. "But because of you and Trevor I knew exactly how to get him to do it."

"Can we not talk about sex, please?" Abby laughed. It was true—every time Abby came home from a date, Lauren had asked very detailed questions. She was relieved that there wasn't any current activity to report.

"Ok, so you're telling me that you've hired Trevor and Claire's love-child to run your website and be your virtual assistant?"

"Can we not call her that?"

"What *do* you want me to call her?"

"She's a person and she has a name. How about Kelsey?"

"Fine." Lauren huffed. "But you can't tell me this isn't weird. It's weird, right?"

"Yes, Lauren. It's weird."

"And what about Trevor?"

"What *about* him?" Abby was feeling more irritated by the minute.

"You know what! How do you feel? I mean, you've been one angry bitch for the last fifteen years!" Lauren rarely minced words.

"Ok, that's not fair. I haven't been a bitch the *whole* time," Abby complained. "I mellowed out after a while. It's just— seeing him stirred everything up again. And I feel bad for him. He's trying to do the right thing. And Kelsey just lost her mother. We both know how that feels."

Lauren got quiet. "I get that but—"

"Do I wish he would have told me about the baby? I don't know. I mean, I probably would have lost my shit. And when Claire moved away, I was honestly relieved. It was easier not seeing her, and she obviously didn't want anything to do with me either. I made a lot of assumptions back then, but now I see the story was way more complicated than I realized."

"As long as you know what you're doing." Lauren's kids started yelling in the background. "Listen, Abbs, I gotta go break up a fight. Have a good night. And be careful!"

"Always."

No sooner did Abby hang up than there was a knock on the door. The conversation with Lauren had raised more questions than answers, and she couldn't get Gil's words out of her head. She looked out the window and saw the colors of the twilight sky reflecting off the Gold Wing's shiny black paint job.

I just can't catch a break, can I?

6
___

She opened the door wide. Trevor was standing with his hands behind his back, looking at the ground.

"You know, this is getting to be a routine and I'm running out of witty things to—"

Before she could finish her sentence, Trevor pulled a helmet out from behind his back. "I found this in my dad's garbage can."

"And that's where it was meant to stay."

"Kelsey told me what happened. She felt awful."

"It's fine. She didn't know. Don't worry about it."

He held out his other hand. In it was a brand-new helmet with the tag still on it—an exact replica of the one Kelsey had broken. It was not a cheap replacement. She'd meant what she told Kelsey about protecting brains, so even her extra helmet was high quality with a dual safety rating.

She took the helmet and shook her head. "You didn't have to do that."

"I know I didn't. But I wanted to." He set the broken one upside down on her porch. "Maybe you can make this one into a planter. It's got good airflow and fairly decent drainage, if you open the vents."

Abby couldn't help but laugh. "Kelsey had a blast on the bike today. Maybe you should keep this so you can take her riding." Abby offered the replacement helmet back.

"I've got one, thanks. Although it's definitely not as nice as this one." He rapped it gently.

She laughed again in spite of herself. "You really didn't have to come over to apologize. Thanks for doing that." She started to shut the door.

"Abby, wait."

She pulled the door back open but was gripping the handle so hard on the inside of the door that her bicep was bulging. Trevor's eyes went there then traveled back to her face.

"Are you mad at me?"

Abby huffed out an audible sigh. "Wow. That's a loaded question. I don't even know how to answer that."

One side of his mouth turned up. "I mean, at the moment."

"You just keep—showing up!" She shook the helmet at him with one hand while still gripping the door with the other. "Can't you just be normal and call or text or something?"

"Well, I might be inclined to do that if you'd volunteer your number, but since this is still enemy territory, I'm treading lightly. You know, erring on the side of being able to run away from the gunshots."

"Yes, but if you called, you wouldn't have to dodge bullets."

"I like to live on the edge."

"Clearly." She started to laugh in spite of herself. "Oh, for God's sake! Just come in or my neighbors are going to start spreading rumors about us."

"And you inviting me in all the time is going to help with that?" He slid past her, made a slight sniffing sound, and let out a contented sigh.

"Quit smelling me!"

"Quit smelling so good!"

She crinkled her forehead, but he just grinned at her.

"See how ridiculous both of those statements are? Neither one of us can help the way we are. Why do you let it ruin your day?" He started to take his coat off. "Why can't *you* just be flattered and let *me* enjoy myself?" His hands gestured back and forth as if there was some sort of simple solution to the impasse between them.

"You're impossible." Abby set the new helmet carefully on the bench by the door and headed for the living room.

"You're all Kelsey's talked about since she got home. I've already heard all about drivers ed, and I'm pretty sure she's studying for her permit right now. I swear she's more excited about riding a motorcycle than driving a car." He hung his coat on a hook and proceeded to unlace his boots.

None of this was lost on Abby.

"They have mud on them," he answered in response to her expression. "Would you rather I track it onto the carpet?"

No, I'd rather you came right out with it and told me what the hell your game is.

When he finally came into the living room, he took a seat in the middle of the couch, which was one square closer than the last time. He took one look at her then held his hands in front of his face as he slid back to the far side. "Don't shoot. I'm unarmed."

"What do you *want*, Trev?"

"Whew!" He made a point of raising his eyebrows and letting his eyes get wide. "Now that? That's a loaded question."

She threw a pillow at him and he dodged it. "You have not grown up one bit, you know that? You're just as goofy as you've always been."

"Now, you see, that's where you're wrong." He leaned back against the cushions, stretched his arms across the back of the couch, and slung one leg up so the ankle rested on the other knee. Abby noticed his neatly rolled jeans and his socks, of all things. They were understated and classy, patterned with yellow and blue paisley and looked exceptionally soft.

He followed her gaze and waved his toes at her. "I *have* grown up. I have a degree, a career, and a plan for my life. I'm still goofy because that's a function of my personality, not my state of maturity. Life should be fun."

Abby sighed. He was right. One of the things she always loved about their relationship was his sense of spontaneity. A simple trip to the grocery store often turned into a trip the grocery store on the coast three towns over because...well, the ocean was there. "You're right. Sorry for being judgy. Now are you going to answer my question or what?"

"I'll take *or what,* if it's on the menu." He waved his toes again.

"It's not."

"And that's why I'm sitting on this end of the couch." He nodded his acquiescence.

"So?"

"You're very hostile today. Did something set you off?"

Abby was so irritated, it was hard to decide where to begin. She put her hands up to her temples. "I just—I wasn't expecting any of this, ok? I came home after three years on the road, and this was supposed to be a month-long recharge for me. I certainly didn't expect to find *you* on my doorstep, or your *daughter* on the back of my bike, or your *dad* whispering in my ear, or—"

"My dad was whispering in your ear?" One of his eyebrows cocked up. "Did he tell you where the money was hidden?"

"This is not a joke, Trevor! This is my life, and you've waltzed in here—" He opened his mouth, but she held up her hand to stop the flow of his words. "And *don't* tell me that's impossible since you're a terrible dancer."

He stifled a laugh with his hand.

"God, you can be so frustrating!" Abby sighed audibly. "You've known about this all along, but put yourself in my shoes. Everything I thought I knew has been called into question. What am I supposed to do with all this new information? I'm going back out for three months of travel, and I don't need my head filled with all these buzzing noises."

He got suddenly quiet and serious. "I'm sorry."

"Well that doesn't help, does it? Those are just words, and they don't take anything back, do they?"

Emotions that had been swirling in her heart came crashing together in the most infuriating way: involuntary, embarrassing tears trickled down her cheeks. It wasn't about today or even the past two weeks. It was about fifteen years of unresolved anger. Fifteen years without closure. She even began to grieve the loss of Claire, which was completely throwing her.

"I lost both of you. At the same time," she said softly. "It was as if you both died in a horrible accident. My two best friends. The two people I trusted most in the entire world."

They stared into each other's eyes for a long time. Neither of them spoke.

"All the apologies in the world can never make that right, Trevor. And that's the bitch of it." She tried to take a breath, but it stutter-stepped its way into her lungs, making a pathetic show of her broken heart.

He slid over to her side of the couch, bullets be damned, and wrapped his arms around her. She struggled at first, but he held her head to his chest and kissed it. "Let me do this, Abby. Let me say it. I *need* to say it. I need you to hear it."

He took her face in his hands. "I'm so sorry. I'm sorry for ruining us. For being an arrogant, black-out drunk who fucked up the only good thing he ever had in his life. But mostly, I'm sorry for hurting the smartest, most beautiful friend and lover I've ever known."

Tears were still running down her face as she listened, and he used his thumbs to wipe them tenderly away, just as Gil had done for Kelsey earlier.

"I've never loved anyone but you, Abby. I've been with other women, sure. But none like you. You've always been the standard." He put his lips to her cheek so gently she could barely feel them, then drew her into his chest.

"I hope you can find it in your heart to forgive me someday." He leaned back into the couch and pulled her with him, stroking the top of her head and breathing in the scent of her.

HER MIND TRAVELED BACK to his dad's garage, before they were together, before he taught her to ride. They were just friends, and she was just a chick who wanted to learn how to wrench on bikes. They were working on an old Royal Enfield his dad had traded for some work. The bike was a classic, and Gil had no idea what he'd been given. He asked Trevor to get it running so he could sell it. Trevor and Abby were taking it apart to see what the problem was. They'd been working on it for days, and still couldn't diagnose the problem. Trevor kept digging deeper until parts were neatly arranged on cloth tarps all over the garage.

Trevor kept talking about it like a bag of gold he'd been handed. He was trying to persuade his dad to let him keep it, but it was worth money. As the days wore on and the garage filled with parts and tools, Gil was starting to get discouraged, until one day he gave up.

He came home from work, parked the car in the driveway for the eighth night in a row and walked into the garage. "I'm starting to think I got the raw end of this deal."

"Don't worry, Mr. Fields. We'll get it running." Abby grinned.

Gil chuckled, giving her a once-over. She was covered in grease and sweat from head to foot. "Well, I appreciate your efforts, little lady, but I'm not so sure."

Trevor looked up. "I'm gonna get it, Dad. You know I will. If I have to go to England and get an owner's manual for this thing, I'm gonna figure it out."

Gil smiled. "How come you can't be this enthusiastic at the shop?"

"I'm not a businessman, I'm a problem solver. I like to fix things. Take them apart and then put them back together."

"We've got a lot of problems you can fix down at the shop, whenever you're ready."

Trevor kept his eyes focused on the bike. "I'll be sure and let you know when that is."

"You do that." Gil nodded politely in Abby's direction. If he'd been wearing a hat, he probably would have tipped it. "Always a pleasure to see your pretty face brightening up this old garage, Abby. You'll be staying for supper, I hope?"

Abby looked at Trevor, and he winked. He didn't seem to care that she was sweaty or greasy, which was fine with her. Being the perfect girl was never her style.

Gil started for the house and then stopped. "I'll tell you what, Trev. If you can get this old bag of bones back together and running, you can have her. Just give me my damn garage back!"

Trevor's face lit up. "Deal."

After his dad closed the door, Abby sat back on her heels. "Trevor, that's amazing! We are *totally* going to get this thing running."

"I like your optimism." He was staring into the cavity left by the carburetor.

"Tell me what I can do next."

"Come here," he said.

She crawled over and peered into the cavity with him. "What do you think?"

"I think I'd like to ask you to dinner some time. Someplace other than my mom's kitchen. Can I do that?"

Dinner? As in, a date? "I don't know, *can* you?"

"What's that supposed to mean?"

"If you use *can,* then it's a question of ability. Like, are you *able* to ask me to dinner. If you want to ask permission, you should use the word *may.*"

"And that technique gets you a lot of dates, does it? Correcting people's grammar?"

She stuck out her chin. "My mother is an English teacher. So sue me."

He kept staring at her mouth, then brushed her cheek from the corner of her lip to her jaw. He started to rub harder.

"What are you doing?" She pulled back.

"You've got grease on your face." He acted like he was concentrating hard on the grease. Then he stopped and leaned in close and said softly, "May I?"

She remembered thinking how sweet it was to ask permission and nodded her approval. Their first kiss was soft and innocent. Then one kiss led to another. When his mother called them in to supper, his parents burst out laughing, because grease was smeared around both of their mouths.

SHE SHOOK HER HEAD, smiling. She hadn't thought about that day in so long.

Trevor dipped his head to look at her face. "What?"

Abby pushed herself up off his chest. "Do you remember that day in your parents' garage, when we got grease all over each other's mouths?"

"Of course I do." He smiled. "My parents never let me live that down."

"I was standing there in your driveway today, talking to your dad, and all these memories came flooding in, and it felt like it was yesterday. And yet at the same time it was like a whole different life, you know?"

He nodded. "It was the same way for me, when I ran into you at Pop's. We have a lot of memories, Abbs. There's no way around that."

"I know, I just—I don't know how to reconcile this. When you showed up at my door a couple weeks ago, I wasn't even going to let you in. I still wonder if it was the right decision."

"I'm so glad you did." He let the words hang in the air for an extra moment, then brushed his fingers ever so gently from the corner of her mouth to the line of her jaw.

"*May* I?"

His breath was warm and soft as he reached for her mouth and pulled her into a kiss. It was slow and deliberate. A reintroduction of sorts. Sweet and careful, his tongue traced the edges of her lips, tasting her, exploring bit by bit.

Abby let her hands slip around him as he took her mouth, remembering for just a moment how it had always felt, being in his arms. Safe. Secure. Like nothing in the world could ever hurt her.

Except him, of course.

Anger had kept her insulated for so long, she'd forgotten what it felt like to be vulnerable. It was strange to think someone could unleash this kind of a storm against her emotional landscape. She tried to adjust to the feeling, but it was just too foreign. It had been too long.

Her heart started racing and she pulled back abruptly. "I can't do this. You have to go."

"I'm sorry. I shouldn't have done that." He slid away from her. "You made it really clear, and I shouldn't have pushed."

"Please, just go. I need you to go now." She closed her eyes and started to rock. *Just breathe, Abby. Don't let this throw you.*

"I don't want to leave it like this."

"Well, you're going to have to, because I need to be alone right now, and I need you to respect that."

"Ok." He stood slowly. "But for the record, this is not my style. I want to figure this out. I want to fix this."

"Just like you fixed that old Enfield?" Her voice was heavy. "That bike was a piece of cake compared to this."

She tucked her legs up, wrapping her arms around her knees. Trevor pulled a blanket off the back of the couch and wrapped her in it, then kissed the top of her head.

"Sleep well, Abby."

Everything was swirling. Love, anger, confusion, longing. He was still lacing up his boots when she called out, "Stop right there. I thought you said this was about Kelsey. This whole thing was supposed to be about her. Getting her through the transition of grief, having her work for me—was that all a game to get you back into my life?"

"No, of course not! I swear, it's not like that. You know me."

"Do I?"

The sounds of boots and laces moving stopped abruptly. "Abby, don't do that. Don't live in the past."

"Then tell me why."

"Can I take my boots off and come and talk to you?"

"I'm pretty sure I can hear you from here."

He slid the helmet over and sat on the bench in the hallway. "I came at first because I wanted you to hear it from me. I didn't want to run into you with Kelsey in the grocery store or at Pop's. I didn't want it to be awkward."

His statement hit her like a brick. "If you saw me at the *grocery store*? That's the best you've got? So in other words, if Claire hadn't died and you never moved back here, you would have never bothered to tell me. Never come back into my life at all. But since your life exploded, *now* suddenly you want to clean up your mess?"

He hung his head, resting his arms against his knees.

Abby's blood was close to boiling. "So basically, you were hedging your bets just in case we ran into each other, is that it?"

"No! I came because I owed you an explanation—and so much more. I came because I've been a coward for all these years, and it was time to own up to the truth."

She pointed her finger in his direction but wouldn't look at him. "You should've led with that. Goodnight, Trev."

"Ab—"

She put her hand up. The conversation was over.

He pulled his coat off the hook and saw himself out. It was a long time before she heard the Gold Wing fire up, but it wasn't until she heard him pull away that the tears began to fall again.

That flight to Santiago couldn't come soon enough.

7

A few days later, on Friday afternoon, Abby got a series of texts from an unknown number:

STILL WILLING TO RIDE TOMORROW?
How bout a picnic in Mendocino?

SHE TYPED BACK:

NICE SLEUTHING, Sherlock.
Or maybe you lifted my number from Kelsey's phone while she slept?

I ACTUALLY HAD it from the voicemail you left me. No heavy lifting required.

. . .

ABBY REMEMBERED the ranting voicemail with a shudder.

MENDOCINO, huh? That's a long ride.

YOUR POINT?

ABBY HADN'T RIDDEN out to Mendocino since the fires had scorched huge swaths of the forest. It had always been one of her favorite stretches of the Pacific Coast Highway, and it would be difficult to see the land decimated like that, but she almost felt a need to pay her respects.

Going back on the road was one thing, but with Kelsey working for her, she was bound to see Trevor from time to time. If she taught her how to ride, even more so. Then what? Was it possible to establish a normal friendship?

Their kiss still had her head spinning. It wasn't like the fire had died down over the last fifteen years. It was a tricky situation, but he wasn't asking for answers to life's looming questions. He was asking about a motorcycle ride.

Running tours, she was always having to take the lead and look out for other riders with varying levels of skill and experience. Road tripping with Trevor had always been so easy. They rode the same way and were wired the same way.

Her mind was caught in a loop of arguments and rationalizations. When she didn't answer, he typed:

MEET you at Pop's for coffee first? KSU @8?

SHE LOVED RIDING first thing in the morning and he knew it.

Kick stands up at eight meant they'd be back by late afternoon and she could still get some laundry done before her trip started on Tuesday. Against her better judgment, she simply answered:

OK.

An early morning ride *and* Mendocino. If he was playing her, he was doing a stellar job. He knew just which buttons to push. She spent the rest of that evening second-guessing herself. It was an unappetizing mix of justification and self-loathing that left an acidic taste in her mouth.

ABBY GOT to Pop's around 7:30 the next morning and slid onto a stool at the long Formica counter. Pop came around and gave her a big squeeze.

"You're up early."

"Yes. Coffee, please!"

"Coming right up." He rounded the counter, grabbing the coffee pot on the way. "Where ya headed?" He poured with one hand and wiped the counter with the other as he spoke. The man was a multi-tasking machine. Short order cooks were like that, and Pop was one of the best.

"Mendocino," she said.

Just then the Gold Wing pulled in, and Pop's face did the math. "With him?"

"Yeah." Abby's expression hardened as she wrapped her hands tightly around the warm cup.

He pointed his finger at her. "You gotta stop freezing him out, ice queen."

"What?"

"You heard me."

Abby's mouth fell open. "Whose side are you on, anyway?"

"I'm on the side of love, darlin'. And *peace*."

"I didn't realize we were at war." She refused to address his use of a word like *love*.

"Sure looks like it from where I stand. Listen, when you get to be old like me, you'll understand. You start seeing things in reverse."

"Reverse?"

He leaned his elbows on the counter and had to take a step back to clear his belly. His gruff, stubbled face, semi-bald head and tattooed chest might have been intimidating to some people, but all she could see was his huge heart beneath it. She respected the hell out of him, which was why she usually listened when he talked.

"I've done a lot of things I'm not real proud of, Abby. Hurt a lot of people. Pain is pretty damn complicated, and anger can be all-consuming, but regret? Regret will eat you alive."

"What do I have to regret? I didn't do anything wrong! I'm the victim here." She kept drinking her coffee as he started wiping again.

"You gotta stop playing that record in your head. You're only a victim if you let yourself be. Now, what *he* did back then?" Pop took that pointer finger and sent it in Trevor's direction. "That's on him. He's gotta live with the consequences, and he's doing a mighty fine job trying, I might add. But your response to all of that?" The finger came right back at her. "How you let it affect *your* life? That's on you and no one else."

"How very Buddhist of you." She didn't even flinch with Pop's big fat finger in her face. She held up her cup and he poured her another splash of hot black liquid.

"All that other stuff is history now. It's just stories about the past. You gotta live inside your own story, not his story."

"Nice play on words."

Pop winked lovingly. "It's the truth, young lady. No way around it."

"Young lady! Am I in trouble?"

"I don't know, are you?"

Abby smirked. "Anyway, what you're talking about is easier said than done."

"Don't I know it?" He pulled another cup, filled it with black coffee, and set it on the counter next to her. "But you're never going to change those facts, and neither is he, so you gotta make a decision." Pop looked up as the door opened. "You gotta start living for today."

Trevor walked in and set his helmet on the counter. "Morning, Pop."

"Morning, Trev. Beautiful day for some throttle therapy."

"That it is. Hey, can we get some lunches in a bag to go?"

"Sure thing."

Trevor sat down tentatively. In a low voice he asked, "Do we need to talk? About the other night?"

"Nope." Abby kept right on sipping her coffee.

"Do you want some breakfast?"

"Nope."

"Are you going to talk to me at all for the rest of the day?"

When their eyes met the showdown began. She was winning too, until the corners of his mouth turned up and his face broke into a smile.

"Yes. Just not until I finish my coffee," she added.

They sat quietly while Trevor pulled out a map and started tracing a route.

"Ever heard of GPS?" She was teasing of course, but it came out more clipped than she intended. Small talk was not one of the ice queen's stronger qualities.

"You know, I have heard of it! It's that little pocket... computer thingy, right?"

Abby tipped her head and smirked.

"I can never get my phone to route me on back roads, even when I tell it to avoid the highways. I like maps. They make me feel like an explorer."

He had that little boy look on his face again and she had to smile. "I'm teasing. I use maps all the time." She was trying to concentrate on the route he'd traced out, but Pop's words kept echoing in her head. "Which way do you want to go?" She tried to sound more chipper.

"How about we circle Clear Lake and maybe grab a snack before heading out to the coast through some of these smaller twisties?" His finger traced the intended route. "Then after lunch we can take the PCH south to Jenner and follow the Russian River through the wine country."

"I am all over that ride." Abby rubbed her hands together in anticipation. "I may even want to stop a few times and get some pictures for my website."

"Absolutely! I'll man the camera and we'll get you in some of the shots with your bike and some great scenery. We'll call it a working trip. You can write it off, you know."

"Not my first rodeo. But thank you, Mr. MBA."

He sipped his coffee and made a face. "Man, that's strong. Hey, Pop! Your coffee is stronger than the fuel in my tank." Pop stood behind the tall counter in the grill area, beaming.

Trevor returned his attention to Abby. "I haven't done a lot of riding over the last few months. It's been a long time since I've ridden out to the coast. Maybe even the last time you and I did it. It'll be nice to get back out on the road." His face softened. "We did a lot of great riding, back in the day. I'm not sure what happened to my sense of adventure. I think it got lost when I did."

And when exactly was that? Abby wondered what the last fifteen years had looked like for him. He and his dad had both used the word *drifted* but that word conjured up images that included dive bars and truck stops, leathered skin and bad teeth. Did he hit bottom and have to climb back up? How bad was it?

"Is that why you do it?" Trevor asked.

"Is that why I do what?"

"Travel. Constant adventure?"

Constant adventure wasn't exactly how she would categorize it, but *continuous travel* was often true enough. Running a business from the road was exciting, but it was also exceptionally difficult. Some days there seemed to be no end to logistical challenges, but she thrived on adventure and wouldn't trade it for any of her previous jobs. The only answer that made sense was that she couldn't get enough miles of open road and wind and freedom. Unfortunately, that made it sound like she was running away, when most of the time she felt like she was running toward something.

Trevor watched her as she tried to form a response, then suddenly it was tumbling out of her.

"The first few years after you left, I did a lot of traveling. I bought my own bike and toured the country. I've been all throughout the continental US and a lot of Canada. But you were right—what you said that first night. After my parents died, something changed in me. I realized how short life is, and how little I knew about the world, so I decided to find out what I didn't know. See what I hadn't seen."

Trevor's attention was fixed on her every word.

"In the process, I realized I wasn't alone. There are so many other women who need to experience life as an adventure. Something to restore their passion and give them a sense of freedom—even if it's just for a week or two. Steel Journeys was born out of that passion—and a hell of a lot of soul-searching."

"I'm proud of you, Abbs. You've done things most people only dream about. Not only that, you've made those dreams possible for others."

"Thanks." She didn't like how sincere he sounded. It was a

lot easier to be mad at him when she put him in the asshole category. "Let's ride, shall we?"

She finished her coffee just as Pop approached with a couple of brown bags. She reached into her pocket, but Trevor was quicker, pulling out his credit card and handing it over.

"Let me get this."

"Ok." Just because he bought her a cup of coffee and a sack lunch didn't make it a date, right? She looked down at his helmet and noticed the Bluetooth headset. It was the same brand as hers so they could pair without a problem. Not that she was a fan of talking during a ride, but it did make communication about photo stops and other vital functions easier. "I have the same kind." She nodded toward his helmet. "We can pair them when we get out to the bikes."

"Sounds good." He grabbed his helmet and they said goodbye to Pop.

"Keep the rubber down and the leather up." This was Pop's standard goodbye.

Outside, Trevor donned his helmet and adjusted the microphone. "Finding good stops for photos might be tricky due to the fires. If I see something I'll tap in and you can do the same." They verified their comms and got settled. "That bike is awful light. You sure it's going to be comfortable for the long ride?" he teased.

"That bike is awful heavy." She returned the volley. "You sure you're going to be able to keep up with me in the twisties?" His laughter was drowned out as she fired up her engine. "Just wait until you see what she can do!"

THEY PULLED AWAY from the diner and took Highway 29. Calistoga was an old town with a rich history that went back hundreds of years. Before the Spanish invaded, the valley north of Napa was home to the Wappo, a peaceful indigenous people. From its quiet appearance, you'd never guess the long and sometimes violent history the region had witnessed. As time unfolded and California was established, the fertile land came to support a mix of vineyards, wineries, and old family farms. The temperate climate made it a rider's paradise of clean roads and varied terrain, sprinkled with natural hot springs.

The ride up to Clear Lake was so different from the landscape she remembered. They wove in and out of areas that had been burned in the wildfires. Some areas were devastated, while others were relatively untouched. The contrast was sobering. A number of ancestral farms had been reduced to ashes, and the land was just beginning to turn over.

Fire and ash are good for the land, she reminded herself. But she couldn't stop tears from streaking out the sides of her eyes and wetting her hair.

She remembered being in Southeast Asia, glued to the tiny news feeds streaming through sketchy phone signals, trying to get updates. Luckily the fires hadn't touched Lauren or her family, but the vitality of many of the surrounding towns had been reduced to rubble, along with their buildings.

Living with constant reminders of loss is just too much for some people, especially if that loss included loved ones. Many chose not to rebuild and left the area completely. Abby understood the kind of loss that drove a person away. Buildings could be repaired or rebuilt, but some things would never be reborn from the ashes.

They pulled up to Clear Lake and settled on a photo stop shortly after the turn onto Highway 20. Trevor came over the intercom and suggested a vantage point with the lake in the background, so she parked the bike and started to dismount.

"Wait. Let me get some of you on the bike first. Just take your helmet off and let your hair flow."

For some reason, his words sent a tinge of electricity down

her spine and it landed right between her legs. She did as he suggested, then watched him pull from his trunk what looked like a beefy digital camera—with a monstrous lens. She wanted to ask where the hell that came from, but he was too far away.

It was curious that he'd come prepared, even though she didn't mention pictures until they were at the diner. Maybe Kelsey had encouraged him? Still, he didn't just pull that gear out of nowhere, and from the way he was handling it, he knew exactly what he was doing. She wondered when he had taken up photography and what the hell he spent time shooting with all that expensive gear.

There was a breeze blowing the hair away from her face, thank God. Otherwise, it would have been a disaster. He walked a little closer and asked her to unzip her jacket a little, his face still planted behind the viewfinder. Again, she did as he asked, wondering just how close of a look he was getting with that lens. She unzipped it slowly, smiling slightly, as she looked right into the camera, teasing him playfully with her eyes.

The shutter snapped before he pulled his face out from behind the lens. "What are you trying to do to me?"

"You asked for it. You give orders like you're on a bikini shoot for *Sports Illustrated*."

"You have a bikini under there? I'm in—let's see it!"

"You're incorrigible."

"Just let me do this. You'll be happy with the pictures, I promise. But no more sexy looks, or you'll be overrun with requests from men wanting to join your tours."

"And women," she added.

"That too," he acknowledged. "Now, let me get a few more angles." He walked around her, sticking his hand inside a case he wore across one shoulder and deftly changing lenses like a nineteenth-century gunslinger.

After a few shots on the bike, he took some of her leaning

over a stone fence and looking out onto the water with her bike in the background.

"When I said we should take some photos for the website, I was thinking candid shots on my smartphone." She was posed the way he wanted, but talking nonetheless.

"Well, we're going to bring your website to the next level," he answered, his face behind the viewfinder, spinning adjustments and looking very professional. He walked over and gently pulled her hair out of her face and laid a strand across her opposite shoulder.

"Where did you learn to shoot?" she asked. He had her turn and lean against the rocks the other way. Once again he posed her, leaning back on her elbows with one of her boots kicked up against the rocks.

He backed up a few paces and didn't answer right away. The shutter clicked a few times before he responded. "A woman I dated for a while. I fell in love with the way her pictures told stories, and I asked her to teach me."

"But you didn't fall in love with *her*?" Abby asked, breaking the pose.

He clicked the shutter one more time before lowering the camera, frustration visible in the jerky movement. "No. I told you already. No."

"You artists are so touchy," Abby teased.

"Let's have a snack," Trevor announced, stowing his gear. Subtlety never was one of his strengths.

"I thought the food from Pop was for lunch."

"It is." He pulled out a few strips of jerky and some dried fruit from one of the side bags. "But I always travel with snacks. You know that."

"It's that bottomless pit of yours," she joked. "I bet you ate a big breakfast before you ever showed up at Pop's."

"Guilty as charged." He took an exaggerated bite of the jerky, and she laughed.

They straddled the wall, facing one another and letting their feet hang on either side. The morning sun was warm as they looked out over the lake.

"Now, that wasn't too painful, was it?" He gestured vaguely to indicate their photo shoot.

"No. Not *too* painful." She watched him for a moment. "Tell me about her."

"Who?"

"The woman who taught you to shoot."

Trevor stopped chewing and blinked in surprise. "No."

"Why not?"

"Because it didn't last, and it didn't mean anything."

"Ok, then. Talk to me about Claire."

"You don't mince words, do you?"

She didn't answer. She just sat there swinging her legs.

"What do you want to know?"

She wanted to know how it happened. How they'd found themselves naked in the hayfield that night. How he could ever think she would forgive him after a stunt like that? But most of all, how he could have the audacity to try to say he didn't remember it? Instead she asked, "Why did you leave?"

"What? When?"

"After it happened." Abby looked away. "Why didn't you fight for me? For us? You just...disappeared."

He stared, incredulous. "We obviously have very different memories of the situation." He took a swig from his water bottle and offered it to her, but she shook her head, waiting for his explanation.

"Abby—I *tried* to talk to you. You wouldn't return my calls."

"I smashed my phone that night after Lauren picked me up. I didn't ever want to talk to either of you again, so I got a new phone with a new number."

"I went to your house so many times. Lauren, your mom,

your dad—everyone kept sending me away. Then I heard through Jake that you went to visit your aunt up in Shasta."

She remembered going to visit Aunt Jane for the summer, but she most definitely did not remember him coming to the house—not once. Abby chewed on her dried mangos, trying to digest everything he was saying. By this time, Trevor's hands were shaking.

"I stopped drinking, like immediately. For the first couple of weeks, I went through horrible withdrawals. When my head finally cleared, I wrote you all those letters. I sent them to your house, I sent them to your aunt's house, but you never responded. I got the message, loud and clear."

He wrote letters? Where were these letters? Did Lauren have them? Did her mother burn them?

"When I got back from Aunt Jane's, you were gone. Both of you. Just gone."

"By then, Claire knew she was pregnant and went to live with her brother's family in Florida. She said she couldn't face you and didn't want you to know about the baby. She made me promise not to tell you, although in hindsight it was a stupid promise I never should have made. She said it was her choice to tell you, not mine. That it was her body. Her business. She left to make a new life and invited me to follow. I didn't go right away. I waited a couple more weeks, but you never came back, and no one would tell me how long you were going to be gone."

They sat quietly for a while longer. Trevor stopped eating and stared out over the water. "Then guilt started to get the best of me. I had fathered a child, like it or not. And I couldn't just leave Claire to figure it out all by herself. I couldn't have lived with myself." He looked up in earnest. "Does that make sense?"

It made perfect sense, actually. He had always been a good guy. Most of the time his problem-solving, fixing-things temperament extended to the people in his life. She was just pissed that it never extended to her. With a child in the picture, it was hard to blame him for doing what was right, even though it did explode her life. If he had walked away from that, she probably wouldn't have respected him either.

"Yeah," she answered simply. "Yeah, it does."

He was right. They had very different memories. Hearing things from his perspective was chipping away at the foundation of anger she had built so long ago.

"I love Kelsey. She's amazing, and I don't know how anyone could let a fuck-up like me be her dad, but I'm doing the best I can. I can't make things right, Abby." He gestured between them. "I accepted that a long time ago. But I need you to know that I wish I could, because I haven't forgotten."

"Forgotten what?"

"This." He gestured between them once again. "You're like my ghost. You've followed me everywhere."

Abby tried to ignore the weight of that statement. "You're not a fuck-up."

"It took me until I was thirty to figure out what I wanted to be when I grew up."

"I think they call that a late bloomer." She threw a stick at him, and he pretended to dodge it.

"You're just being nice. Your mother was right to hate me."

"She didn't hate you," Abby lied. "She just didn't think you were good enough for me."

"Turns out she was right." He winked as he said it. "Look how well you've done without me."

Trevor's parents liked Abby. She spent a lot of time at their house, but that was mostly because her parents didn't approve of Trevor. Her father sneered at him all the time, and her mother was constantly harping about that boy on the motorcycle. It didn't help that she was a teacher and he'd failed too many classes in his last semester of senior year to graduate. In fact, when her mother found out about Trevor's betrayal, she tried to forbid Abby to see him, which was laughable because

Abby was twenty-one at the time. It was Mom's idea for Abby to spend that summer in Shasta.

Come to think of it, that whole summer was a blur. She remembered sitting on her aunt's rope swing and wondering what she was going to do with the rest of her life. All her plans had been *him*, and that wasn't right, her aunt told her. "You need to figure out what Abby wants, who Abby wants to be."

THE BREEZE WAS BLOWING JUST ENOUGH to make tiny waves lap against the shore of the lake. It was quiet and peaceful. Time stood still just long enough to give them a moment of vulnerability.

"Hey, Trev?"

"Yeah?"

"I never got any letters."

"What?" The look on his face went from surprise to shock. "You're kidding me, right?"

She shook her head. "I wish I were. I wish I had known you still cared."

"Still cared? Abby, I wanted to marry you!"

Hearing those words sliced through time and reopened the wound. Convincing herself that he didn't care had been the only way to reconcile such an enormous amount of grief and pain. With a combination of apathy and indignation she concocted a balm to protect what was left of her broken heart. Now, she sat quietly, taking it in, wondering what it meant.

"It would have never worked, Trevor. I wasn't mature enough to accept the truth and let you stick around. Hell, I'm having trouble with it even now."

"Maybe so," he replied. "But I can't stop thinking about the way it was supposed to turn out. It was really shitty how everything went down."

"Really shitty," she agreed.

"What do you suppose your mom did with all those letters?"

"I really don't have any idea," she said in a small voice, "and it's too late to ask her. But it's not too late to ask Aunt Jane."

"Let me know if you do. I'll watch for the eruption coming from Shasta."

"Aunt Jane never hated you." Abby laughed. "She just hated watching me go through all of that. She hated that I didn't know how to be my own person without you." She didn't mean for that last part to come out.

"I'm not sure what to believe anymore." His eyes were pleading.

"Me neither." This puzzle had been solved and boxed up long ago, or so she thought, and these extra pieces presented an unwelcome challenge. She swung her legs inside the wall. "Let's ride."

"I like the way you think, Abby Steel."

They circled Clear Lake before heading out Highway 20 to the coast. Mendocino was stunning any time of year, but fall was one of Abby's favorites. Endless miles of bucolic, rolling vineyards were dotted with trees full of reds, oranges, and yellows, ending in rocky cliffs that dropped off into the spectacular blue of the Pacific Ocean. It didn't get any better or more beautiful than this particular stretch of coastline.

Trevor didn't use the comms much, just a little smack talk from time to time—whose bike was better, faster, easier to ride. Sometimes she listened to meditation music, but her taste in music varied widely now, and her playlists were a hodgepodge of songs she'd captured along the way. In Northern California, none of the new music felt like it fit, so she just turned it off, thankful for the quiet. She needed the miles to sort through the tangle of emotions that wound around her heart.

Abby loved all kinds of bikes, for all kinds of reasons, but when she needed to think, nothing beat the constant hum of a

Harley's V-Twin on a cleanly paved road. Every mile loosened the knots, and rounding each curve helped her navigate the maze.

Before they got to Mendocino, Trevor fired up the comms and turned on his blinker. "Ready to stop for lunch?"

"Sure," Abby replied.

They pulled off onto a side road that worked its way up into the headlands, ending at the top of a hill on what looked like an old, deserted farm road. Trevor parked his bike near a tree and took off his helmet, closing his eyes as he turned his face up to the sky. The air was crisp and clean coming off the ocean.

When he finally opened his eyes, Abby was smiling at him. "What?"

"You wouldn't be so keen on taking deep breaths if you could smell some of the places I've been."

Trevor laughed.

"I swear you're part bloodhound. If we were lost in the wilderness, I'll bet you could pick up the scent of a trail that would lead us home."

He sniffed several times for effect. "God didn't make it this big for nothing!"

"That is *not* a big nose."

"Well, it's not small, I'm just saying."

"This place is beautiful. How'd you find it?"

"A buddy of mine owns that vineyard there." He pointed to the south side of the hill.

"Hence the plethora of *Private Property* and *No Trespassing* signs?" Abby laughed. "Does he know you're up here?"

"He brought me here once, and I was just floored by the view. I told him that if I owned this property, I'd build my house on this exact spot. He said that I was welcome to all the view I could stand."

"I guarantee some employees on four-wheelers will be kicking us out any minute," Abby joked.

"It used to be the only access road for this side of the property, but eventually they built other roads that connect straight to the main buildings, so no one ever uses this one anymore."

"Well, aren't you full of interesting facts?"

"You know what else I'm full of?"

"Yes. Yes, I do." She laughed.

8

Trevor pulled their lunch bags, a small cooler, and a blanket from his trunk and side bags. "I mean, look at all this storage space! Whose bike do you like now, huh?"

Abby shook her head and followed him onto the hillside to a soft patch of grass, where he laid the blanket out in the warm September sun. He stripped off his leathers, his boots, and his socks. Abby took her chaps and jacket off and balled them up on the blanket, neither one of them saying much.

Trevor sat like a little kid, squishing his toes in the grass. He loved touching the grass with his bare feet. It was another one of those strange idiosyncrasies that were just...Trevor. Come to think of it, he didn't much like shoes at all.

The vista was spectacular, so they sat taking it in, the distant ocean a perfect backdrop. Abby took her shoes off too. It was something she'd started doing in pretty much every country she visited. She liked the idea of connecting with the earth in a new place and introducing herself to the land.

Seeing their bare feet sticking up from the end of the blanket, she realized this was a habit that didn't actually belong to her. She'd learned it from him all those years ago. There were so many memories of them lying side-by-side, with their feet to the elements, talking about life.

"What's for lunch?" she asked, sitting up.

"I don't know." He reached for the bags and tossed her one. "I didn't bother to look."

As she went to open the brown paper sack, she saw writing scribbled on it. "Hey—this one's yours." She grinned, pointing to the grease-pen letter T smeared on one side of the bag.

He laughed, turning his bag over, only then noticing the big letter A. "Well, let's see what Pop has in store for us this time."

After they switched bags, Abby found a tuna sandwich on rye bread with a whole pickle and a bag of salt-and-vinegar chips. "He loves me." She feigned a swoon before biting into her sandwich.

Trevor sat watching her eat, to the point where it started to get uncomfortable. His eyes traveled past her face to the hills behind her, then all around her body, as if he was framing her picture in his mind's eye.

"What are you doing?"

"Nothing." He dove into his bag, wearing an extremely happy expression when he pulled out a double turkey club on whole wheat, a bagel with cream cheese, and an apple.

"Hey, I'll trade you that apple for these chips."

"What is this?" Trevor slapped his chest, aghast. "Abby Steel is giving away salt-and-vinegar potato chips?" He looked around excitedly. "Am I on a game show?"

"It's not that big a deal. I just eat healthier these days. My body thanks me for it."

He took a second to scan her figure, then tossed her the apple. "No complaints here."

God, he was charming. It was absolutely irritating how charming he could be. The way he watched her always made her feel soft inside, something that hadn't happened in a very long time. Her outer shell might be hard, like a helmet, but one good fall and its integrity could no longer be trusted.

"Tell me about your tours." He lay back down on his jacket.

"What do you want to know?"

"I studied business, so tell me about your business. I mean, how do you plan the rides? How do you organize everything?"

"Honestly? I have a really good accountant, great business software, and I communicate with people through groups on the internet. Each group has its own dedicated site where we can get to know each other in the weeks leading up to the ride. That's how I share most of the information as well. I used to do it all through email, but groups are better, because the riders often answer each other's questions, and all those questions used to come directly to me. We're talking like the same exact question from five different people." Abby shook her head. "It's been a life-saver."

"Where's the very first place you went with a group?"

"Vietnam."

"That must have been so beautiful. And you'd been there before?"

Abby nodded. "Most of the places I've been to at least once, but I still go about ten days early and ride the route again. I check in with the accommodations, and make sure everything is in order before the groups arrive. Helps to avoid surprises. It also gives me a chance to get some good solo rides in. I take a lot of notes and pictures and catalogue them by country and season."

"I'd love to photograph some of those rides. Think you'd ever let a dude ride along?" He looked over hopefully.

"Not likely. Although, I'm sure you're a much better photographer than I am."

"Speaking of which..." He pulled himself up onto one elbow. "Do you mind if I grab the camera and get some more shots of you next to your bike? Perched on top of this hill with the sweeping views...it'll look great on your website."

She studied him. "Why are you being so nice?"

"What do you mean?"

"To me. Why are you being so nice to *me*?"

Trevor's eyebrows went up. "First of all, I don't know what you're talking about, because I'm just being myself. But second, I already told you." He looked deep into her eyes, repeating the sentiments he'd expressed out loud. "How could you even ask a question like that?"

He still loved her. She could see it in his eyes, his expression. She took a bite of the apple and turned away, pretending to focus on the view. It was hard to look at him without everything barreling back at her.

He was right. It wasn't a fair question.

Being himself was what Trevor did best. He'd always been kind and thoughtful. It may not have been what attracted her in the first place, but it had definitely kept her in the game. He was never a mean drunk, just a horny one, and that never used to bother her. Right up until the day he crossed the uncrossable line.

It was hard to fault him for being honest. It was also hard to fault him for trying to pick up the pieces and build a life for Kelsey. It was the right thing to do and he was doing it. When she looked over at him, his face was soft. Quiet. Patient. He wasn't playing her. Not at all. He was being sincere, and that was all it took.

Her outer shell cracked, and her icy heart began melting in the afternoon sun. She let her eyes trail up his body lying next to her on the blanket. She looked at his broad chest, and when their eyes met, she watched his face register what was happening.

He lifted himself up onto his arms to bridge the distance between them but didn't say a word. Abby reached out to place a hand on his chest, and when she touched him, his breath sucked in. She traced a line down his middle, stopping just above his belly button, then tucked her hair behind one ear and drew her eyes up to meet his gaze.

Memories began to seep in through the cracks. Memories of making love with him on blankets like this, on beaches and in meadows and under trees. Making love outdoors had been one of their things and it still thrilled her to think about the air blowing across their naked skin. She wondered briefly if he'd brought her here because of it, but the thought dissolved with the rest of her arguments when he reached up and pulled her face to his.

This time there was no need for an introduction. Their bodies remembered precisely what to do. He wrapped her in his arms and they fell back onto the blanket and into one another. Abby silenced every argument, every doubt, every fear, and gave herself to him. She was leaving for three months, and even if it was just this one time and never again, it was worth it to feel his passion again, to remember what it felt like to be truly loved.

They lay on the blanket for a long time, anticipating the throttle but leaning into the curves, with long wet kisses fueling their want. She tugged his white T-shirt out from the waistband of his jeans, running her hand up under it and letting her fingertips gently explore the soft skin on his abdomen. He sucked on her neck and the hollow space under her collarbones and then returned to her mouth.

The Trevor she used to know would have had her shirt off already, but this older, wiser version of Trevor had style and finesse. He was taking his time, kind of like that night on the beach from the photograph, only much, much better.

Abby was so ready for a man who knew how to drive. So many of her sexual encounters had been spent on men who were greedy and fast but got the job done. Being with Trevor was like being pulled into a trance.

He laid her back and slowly pulled her shirt out of her pants and shimmied it up to her ribs, placing soft kisses along her stomach as he went. Leaving her shirt where it was, he reached over, intertwining their hands and pulling their one mutual fist up to his lips. He began sucking on her fingers one by one, sliding them in and out of his mouth, and licking them slowly with his eyes closed.

She watched him with wonder. Pictures of the past that felt blurry and underdeveloped collided with the present view. Maybe it had taken him this long to grow into the man he was supposed to be. Maybe the best of Trevor was right now. Or still to come.

In Tanzania she'd met a wise old healer who told her that life was merely a mirage. We tell ourselves what we want to see, he said, and so that's what we see, but it doesn't ever bring us the satisfaction we truly need.

She had loved Trevor so intensely, and then shut him out so completely, that the resulting fracture distorted her view. She tried to see him now, in the moment, as he was—as a man who wanted to show her his love in a deep and tangible way, if only she could let him.

He pulled his shirt over his head and removed his belt, his body looming above her, tanned and beautiful. Abby wanted to take her shirt off as well but was curious to see what this newfound maturity had brought to Trevor's lovemaking, so she let him drive for a while longer.

Her chest moved heavily as he lowered himself down onto her, their stomachs touching for the first time, lighting a fire deep in her belly. He stopped just shy of a kiss and looked her in the eye.

"I love you, Abby." He reached up and put a finger over her mouth so she wouldn't respond. "I know I didn't have to say that but I want to. I want you to know that *before* we make love, not after. I'm not a child anymore, and my feelings for you have nothing to do with sex. But I *am* going to make love to you."

He was no longer asking permission. It was no longer necessary. His breath was coming in shorter bursts. "And I'm going to take my time, because I've imagined this moment over and over again, and I don't want to miss a thing."

He moved his finger and covered her lips with his mouth instead. It wasn't necessary. She had no desire to argue. Not with the heat of his skin lighting her insides on fire. All she could hear were his words ringing in her ears and birds in the trees and distant sounds of farm equipment. The sun was warm and they were on a slow burn and that was just fine with her.

He pulled away and watched his own hand trailing the length of her waist. Slowly he went, and it made her shiver. His eyes moved across her face as a tear fell from the corner of one of her eyes. He reached up and brushed it away.

"Are you ok? Do you want me to stop?"

Not something the old Trevor would have even *thought* of saying.

"No. God, no." She sucked in some air. It was hard to look him in the eye and admit the truth at the same time. "I haven't been touched like this since...well, since the last time you touched me, I guess."

"We're going to have to do something about that." Sliding his hand down past her waist, he wrapped it around her pelvic bone, pulling it toward him and locking them together for just a moment, letting her feel how hard he'd become. "I've had a few lessons since we were together last. I can't wait to show you what I've learned."

He dipped his head and softly kissed her neck. Pulling her into an embrace, he whispered in her ear, "Whatever you do, Abby, whatever happens, don't regret this moment."

When he pulled away, she ran her fingers across his

muscled torso, feeling his back flex with the effort it took to hold himself back.

She stopped time, reaching up to stroke his cheek. "Here, in this moment, everything else is gone. It's just you and me. I want you to take me. I want you to consume me."

It had been so long since she'd been able to say words like that. Since she'd felt the pull of desire that could dredge those words to the surface. Over the years, sex had become less about the experience and more about necessity, but with Trevor everything was backward. This was not a necessity—far from it —but the need for him called to her from someplace deeper than her groin. Deeper than logic could explain.

He slid his knee in between her legs and pushed one thigh out of the way so that he could press into her. Even with two pairs of jeans between them, the heat was intense.

It felt like slow motion when he finally lifted her shirt over her head, cupping a breast in one hand and kissing the top of it as it mounded inside her bra. He effortlessly slipped one hand behind her and threw the clasp but was gentle and attentive as he helped her slip out of it, openly admiring her shape and how hard her nipples had become in the breeze. He lowered onto one elbow beside her and ran his fingers over her chest as if reading braille, then followed with his tongue, which made her back arch involuntarily.

He stayed there, enjoying her body for what seemed like hours, gently exploring the underside of each soft breast before continuing to the soft part of her stomach. The wetness of his tongue left a trail that made her skin tingle as the breeze moved across it, and it was all she could do to keep from flipping him over and taking him right there. Each time she wondered how much more she could take, he changed tack just slightly, drawing out her desire, and holding her captive to the pleasure he invoked.

He unbuttoned her jeans, revealing the tattoo on her hip,

then stopped, fingering the artwork. He didn't say anything; he just traced the outline where it met her curves and slid her jeans past her hips.

"A thong. Nice choice. Was that for me?" He smiled.

"No," she replied, squirming a little. "It's more comfortable on long rides—it helps my legs not to fall asleep."

He ran one finger under the top edge of the delicate purple lace, pulling it away from her skin slightly and once again following with his tongue. "Well, I'm sorry, but this is not an image I'm ever going to get out of my head now."

He pulled her pants the rest of the way off and took a moment to set them aside. The restraint he showed was almost maddening. She could feel herself literally starting to drip.

He lifted one of her legs and ran his hand along the inner thigh, stopping just shy of the thong. "You say you don't get touched like this. Why not?"

The truth? She never let anyone close. Sex was on her terms and that was it. She took what she needed and never let anyone in. Abby wasn't sure if he was actually looking for an answer or if he was just stalling, because he proceeded to hook his fingers into the sides of her thong and shimmy it down her legs.

He didn't wait for an answer, and when he spread her legs to taste her, she just about exploded. He took the time once again to introduce himself, slowly exploring until her breath was ragged and she could barely lie still.

"Why don't you just let go of all that delicious tension, Abby? Let me take care of you."

When he really started in, it was like nothing he'd ever done before. This new, refined technique was a thousand times better, and it wasn't long before she came with an intense release that left her shaking and out of breath.

But that was just the beginning. He slid out of his own pants and brought his naked body up on top of hers to calm the shaking, to hold her and kiss her and bring her back from the edge momentarily. She could feel him firmly set between her thighs and ached to have him inside her. He reached for a condom and she breathed into his neck.

"Trevor. I've missed you."

"I've missed you too. I can't tell you how much." He kissed her forehead, her neck, and her chest before returning to her lips. "I'm going to show you instead."

He directed himself deep inside her, sliding slowly to the base of his shaft, and let out his own soft cries of pleasure. Abby began to roll her hips in time with his movements until they found their rhythm. Intense and beautiful, time stood still as they savored the moment, riding the waves, letting them swirl out of control and then bringing them back.

She kept expecting him to just take what he needed, but instead, once again, he surprised her. In one sweeping motion he rolled her on top of him, letting her find a rhythm of her own. He watched her as she moved, the sun lighting up her skin and her hair blowing in the breeze. He got that look again, like he was framing a picture.

Too many years of bad sex had only one upside—she had learned how to please herself without throwing a man over the edge. They started a long, easy climb to the top of a very high mountain before it broke for both of them and their cries mingled down the hillside and echoed off the canyon walls.

Abby collapsed into his chest, breathless and spent. He wrapped her in his arms, pushing her hair out of the way so he could kiss her cheek. "You're gorgeous. Being with you has always been magical."

She snuggled in beside him, laying her head on his chest. He pulled one edge of the blanket over her as they settled in. Trevor had never been a roll-over-and fall-asleep kind of guy. They used to lie together for hours, talking about their hopes and dreams. They had even talked about having kids and teaching them to ride and to love the outdoors.

"It must have been hard for you," she said softly.

"What's that?" He pulled his jacket under his head for a pillow.

"Having Kelsey but not being able to teach her how to ride or take her on adventures."

He was quiet for a while. "Yeah, well—for a long time I wasn't exactly a stable enough figure to warrant the privilege. You're right though. I'm pretty sure that up until now, the biggest outdoor adventure of her life was coming here from Florida in a moving van."

"Well, we're going to have to do something about that."

"We?"

"Hold the reins there, cowboy. It's just an expression. I'm not the one sticking around in her life. It's up to you to decide what her new normal is going to be—and how much change she can adjust to at a time."

"She said you agreed to teach her to ride."

"And I will—three months from now, when I get back. You know better than anyone it's the day-to-day stuff that makes life into an adventure, and you're the best person I know to teach her that."

"Thank you. That's very nice of you to say." He gave her a playful squeeze.

"Yeah, well—don't spread it around. It'll ruin my rep. I'm the ice queen, you know."

"What? Who calls you ice queen?"

"Pop. He said it this morning."

Trevor's chest jiggled as he laughed. "Well, we're going to have to do something about that too."

"I think you already did. I'm pretty sure I melted all over your blanket."

"Yeah. Scoot over, would you?" He made a show of pretending to push her out of the way.

"You want me to wash it at my place? Kelsey doesn't need to

wonder why you're bringing home a blanket that smells like sex."

"Oh, shit. I didn't think about that. There's so much to worry about with teenagers. Yeah, I guess so. If that's ok."

"You're not the only one who needs to save face. I don't want her knowing about this any more than you do."

"I'm not really worried about her knowing about the sex, although the blanket is probably over the edge, even for me."

"You're not worried? Even with Claire gone so recently?"

"It wasn't like that between me and Claire—not that she would remember. Anyway, I think she'd be ok with it."

Abby thought about Kelsey's comment at the diner, about how she knew they'd been in love once.

"I'm certainly not ashamed of being given another chance to be with you," Trevor continued. "But I don't want her concept of what this is or isn't to put pressure on us."

She wondered just how many times Claire and Trevor had sex, and it started to get in her head. "And what do you think this is? Or isn't?" She was starting to get worried. Worried about having let herself go. Worried about how this would complicate her life.

"Don't do that."

"Do what?"

"Start regretting."

He was right. His body was warm and comforting, and she didn't want to cheapen the experience, but still, they couldn't force this into something it wasn't.

"To answer your question, I'm not trying to figure anything out right now. I wasn't expecting this to happen, so I'm just lying here trying to be grateful for an incredible experience with a beautiful woman I care very deeply about. *And* who has an incredible body," he teased, sliding his hand over her hip. "Your skin is better than any curve I've ever ridden. I could touch you all day." He sighed heavily for effect. "But then we'd have to sleep out here, and I only have this one blanket, and it would be too cold and—"

"I can see the coast from here," she interrupted. "I'll bet they have hotel rooms in Mendocino."

"Wait—what?"

"I'm not propositioning you. I'm just saying, we're not broke twenty-somethings anymore. If the day gets away from us, we can just grab a room."

"Roger that." He smiled, leaning his head on his jacket again. "And now, back to living in the moment." He continued rubbing his hand over her hip and the silence stretched between them. "It's not going to be easy. There's a lot wrapped up in this."

"I know," she said quietly. There would be plenty of time for a post mortem while she was out on the road again.

"Was it always that good?"

"Was *what* always that good? The sex?" she asked.

"Yes."

Abby thought about that for a minute. "I don't think so. I don't think I knew enough back then. It was always special because you were my first and we were just two kids figuring it out, and everything was new and different and wonderful. But did it ever feel like that? No way. Not even close."

"Well, you certainly know enough now." He squeezed her waist and it made her jump.

"Bad sex is a good teacher." She laughed, slapping his chest.

"True that."

"You too, huh?"

"Mm-hmm." He was stroking her hair and breathing deeply. "You smell amazing."

"I guess some things never change, huh?" She pinched the skin on his abdomen.

"Hey! Stop that." His grabbed onto her hand, pulling it up with astonishing speed.

"Wow. I don't remember those lightning-fast reflexes." She looked up at him. "Where'd you pick those up?"

"Never you mind. Let's just enjoy the sunshine, shall we?"

"Fine." Her eyes narrowed. "But just try and see if you can keep your little *Fight Club* secrets from me!"

"Uh-huh."

THE SUN WAS warm and the breeze was light. She held his chest and snuggled into the blanket, with more questions than answers running through her mind. It was hard not to wonder what it all meant, but she wanted to take this memory with her, untainted. She tried to push everything aside and be in the moment.

When she looked through her rose-colored glasses, she imagined being in a modest hotel room in Argentina, drifting happily to sleep alongside hazy warm memories of an afternoon of lovemaking in the sun. When she took those glasses off, however, she saw herself day-drinking and beating herself up for being stupid enough to open this enormous can of worms.

The truth was probably somewhere between the two. Or worse, the tortuous flip-flopping that was indicative of the never-ending war between her heart and her mind.

Suddenly, images flashed in her vision—a knight in full armor on a horse with a jousting pole, headed straight at her. She braced herself for the impact and the next thing she knew he had her heart on the end of his jousting pole, dripping with blood, but still beating. She didn't feel any different, with her heart separated from her body like that, and it was strange to think that she couldn't tell the difference. She looked up again at his jousting pole and watched her heart turn to a chunk of blue ice and break off in pieces, falling down around him.

The knight raised the visor on his helmet to take a closer

look at the pieces that now lay on the ground, and just as he turned his face to look at her, she opened her eyes. She was still on the blanket with Trevor, but the sun was in a different position in the sky. She jiggled Trevor's arm. "Hey! Wake up! I think we fell asleep."

"Yeah." He blinked a couple of times. "I guess so."

"I suppose we should get a move on. We're burning daylight."

"Ok. Yeah." He pulled out his phone. "Oh, that's not good."

"What?"

"It's already three o'clock. I should text Kelsey and let her know it's going to be a lot later than I thought."

"Look at you, being all parent-like. Do you need to go home?"

"Not on your life." He started texting. "This is a perfect day. And I'm going to enjoy every minute of it."

"So much for being parent-like."

"Don't worry! She's with her grandparents right now, and she has a sleepover at a friend's house tonight. I'll just let her know that I won't see her before she goes, but I'll pick her up in the morning."

Fuck it. If he could throw caution to the wind and enjoy the day, so could she. "Perfect! I haven't seen a California sunset in ages."

Trevor went over next to a tree and peed. When he turned around Abby started laughing hysterically.

He put his hands on his hips. "You know, laughing at a man's nakedness does *not* instill a lot of confidence." He smiled, unashamed, and walked back over. "What the hell is so funny?"

She touched the left side of her face a few times. "Oh my God. It's happened again, Trev."

"What has? Will you *please* tell me what you're laughing at?"

"You're sunburned. But only on the right side of your body."

"What are you talking about?" He looked down at his arms

and legs, then looked at the blanket. "Oh, shit!" He burst out laughing. "You were lying on me, and the blanket was covering... Holy fuck, that's funny!"

"I'm assuming the left side of my face is burned as well?" She was still touching the skin there, which felt hot and tight.

He shaded her with his hand, kneeling to get a closer look. "I'm afraid so." He kissed her cheek gently.

"Then we're outed." She smiled at him. "Just like the grease smears from your garage."

"I guess so."

"I was hoping this could be our little secret." Abby sighed. "There's no way I'm going anywhere near your parents." She fell over on the blanket, covering her face with her hands. "Why do I feel like a teenager again? I'm thirty-six years old, for God's sake! I should be able to fuck whoever I want to."

"We do have a way of making interesting memories, don't we?" He slapped her ass. "Come on, let's ride. There's nothing we can do about it now."

She looked over at the food. "There's no way I'm eating the rest of that tuna after it baked in the sun for two hours."

"Agreed. Let's pitch this and grab a bite in Mendocino."

Trevor packed the bike as she excused herself.

"Your clothes cover most of the burn. But our faces are hilarious," she said, walking out from behind a tree.

"Could be worse. At least my dick was covered." He winked. "Don't worry. It'll turn to tan in a couple of days."

"Speak for yourself, Mr. Florida. This is going to be a nightmare for my pale white skin. At least you don't peel."

"Yeah but *this* is not going to be comfortable," he said, wincing, as he pulled the helmet over his head.

"I've ridden with more pain than this. Don't be a wuss."

"I'm just saying a brain bucket might be nicer than the full face at this point." He buckled his strap gingerly. "More pain? When? What happened?"

"It's a long story. I'll tell you on the way." She fired up her bike and turned it around easily, while it took Trevor a few gyrations to get the big Gold Wing facing down the hill instead of up. She took the extra time to look for a restaurant to try in Mendocino, then hit the button on their intercoms. "Whose bike do you like now, huh?"

"Very funny."

9

They rode Highway 20 until it ended almost at Fort Bragg, then turned south on the PCH. It was a lot colder on Highway 1 than Abby remembered, so she switched on her grip heaters and closed the vents on her helmet. She wasn't about to catch any shit for being cold from a guy with full fairings and a heater.

Mendocino was just as beautiful as she remembered, with low buildings perched on jagged cliffs that dropped off into the ocean. They pulled into a mom-and-pop eatery that looked warm, cozy, and casual, and waited until they got inside to remove their jackets. He pulled out her chair and they ordered some coffee.

"There's a restaurant I want to try called The Ravens, but we're definitely not dressed for it." Not to mention it was attached to a hotel, and she didn't want to be tempted to spend the night with him.

"Maybe some other time," he said hopefully.

They ordered soup and sandwiches, and the server looked at them funny when she noticed their faces. "You guys...both fell asleep in the sun facing in opposite directions?"

"More like facing each other." Abby smiled. "It's weird, right?"

"Well—" she tipped her head sideways— "if you put your faces together it would look right. In either direction, I guess." She walked around each of their chairs. "I don't know. I just hope you don't peel only on the one side, or you'll end up looking like that villain from the Batman movies."

Trevor raised his eyebrows. "You mean Two-Face?"

"Yeah! Yeah." She nodded. "I'm sorry, was that rude? I mean, not that hideous or anything." Her face got progressively pinker. "I'm gonna go put this order in."

She walked away quickly, clearly embarrassed, and they both started laughing.

"Oh. My. God." Abby shook her head. "And this from a complete stranger! What are your parents going to say? What's *Kelsey* going to say?"

"That depends. But you're right—we probably shouldn't be seen together until our faces go back to normal."

"Man, it's stressful being back in the States! I feel so hyper-aware of how I look." She tossed her napkin on the table. "I'm going to the restroom. I need to check this out in a real mirror."

"You look beautiful!" Trevor called after her, chuckling at her irritation.

When she came back, she found him looking at himself through the camera on his phone. "It's not so funny when you really look at it, is it?"

He lowered the phone. "No, it's still pretty damn hilarious. Should we jet off to South America and hide in the jungle for a while until our skin evens out? I've always wanted to wear those big, wide-brimmed hats."

"That's not a bad idea." She took her seat. "But I'm already one step ahead of you." At this point, the fact that she was leaving was part grief and part relief.

"When do you leave?"

She could see the hesitation in his face, but facts were facts. "Next Wednesday."

"Four days." He took a deep breath and nodded. "And you come back when? Three months this time?"

"I haven't booked my return ticket, but approximately, yes. I have tours planned in Argentina and Chile, plus Brazil and Costa Rica. The last one ends in late January. I was thinking about heading to Belize after that for a little R & R on the beach, since it'll still be cold here. Maybe come back around the first of February to regroup."

Trevor simply nodded. At least they were no longer teenagers dealing with the drama of separation, regardless of how they might feel about one another. Trevor was forthcoming about his feelings, but Abby's heart felt trapped between a beautiful and terrible past and an uncertain, improbable future.

"How's your Spanish?"

"I get by. It gets easier when I'm in country surrounded by Spanish speakers," she explained. "Sometimes I have to hire an interpreter, like East Asia and Eastern Europe, but in South America, Brazil has been my biggest challenge. Portuguese is an exceptionally difficult language."

"It's really incredible, what you're doing. You know that, right?"

Was it really so incredible? Or was it simply the life she'd built—part of the shell that had been insulating her all these years? "Thanks," she replied, not knowing what else to say.

"I'm pretty sure you're Kelsey's hero, so she'll be waiting on those riding lessons."

He was being nice again, and a little distant. Then again, how could she blame him? It was going to be awkward, no matter how it went down. It wasn't going to be easy to file this experience, like so many others, in the *does not matter* category. The fact was, it did matter, more than she was willing to admit.

She had to remind herself that one sexual encounter after fifteen years did not a relationship make. She might have to remind Trevor too.

"Show me some of your pictures," he said.

"Of what?"

"I don't know. Do you take group photos? Let me see some of these women who choose to come out with you for weeks at a time and explore foreign lands on motorcycles."

Abby tapped around on her phone until she found the folder with group photos from the past two years. She handed it to Trevor, and he began to scroll.

"Steel Journeys is a great name," he said, still looking at the phone. "What a bunch of badass women! You're like the *Charlie's Angels* of motorcycles, without the misogynistic overtones of course." He laughed, handing the phone back. "You should call yourselves the Bitches of Steel."

Abby head tilted. She was deep in thought.

"Get it? It's a play on your name. Like a gang with you as the leader, but in a very cool, non-threatening way."

"Hmm."

"Did I say something wrong? Because I was just messing around. You know, how it's not politically correct for me to call a woman a bitch, but women call themselves badass bitches all the time—and with pride."

The server brought their food and Abby finally started nodding. "No, no. I actually like that. I think it could work! There's a double entendre too, because bikes are made of steel, and there's already steel in the name of the company."

"Exactly!" He took a bite of his sandwich and then put it down, leaning in with a quieter voice. "These sandwiches ain't got nothing on Pop's."

They talked about her company a bit more, trying to avoid small talk but not doing a very good job. It was going to be about two-hours of riding on Highway 1 until they turned inland through the Russian River Valley. That would put them at just about sunset before they left the coast.

"What do you think about our timing?" he asked as they headed out to their bikes.

"Talk about a loaded question."

Trevor rolled his eyes. "I mean sunset and the length of ride we still have to go."

"I know what you meant. Let's just play it by ear, ok? It would be a shame to miss what's probably going to be a spectacular display. It should only be an hour to get home after that. I don't mind riding in the dark, if you don't."

"It'll be pretty squirrely through some of those first sets of curves, but once we hit Forest Hills it should straighten out."

"Don't you worry about me. My bike loves the curves." She wiggled her body in big S curves like a snake.

He watched her move and when their eyes met, she could see the want in them all over again. Her body responded in kind, and she swallowed. "Sorry."

He looked away, rubbing a hand across his chin. "Are you going to be warm enough?"

He said it sincerely, but she couldn't help feeling amused. "I've got heated gear. Don't you worry about me." She proceeded to pull her jacket liner and gloves out of the saddle bags and put them on.

"Yeah, me too." Trevor just switched on his heater and winked. "Whose bike do you like now?"

"Still mine," she replied. "I can put the gear on or take it off, but I still have more fun on the curves than you ever will."

"Maybe you'll let me ride it someday?"

"Sure thing. Just as long as you don't make me drive that pig." It was all in good fun. She'd spent many hours on the back of bikes just like that with Trevor, way before she rode her own.

"I don't suppose you ever ride bitch anymore."

"Nope."

In fact, she hadn't been a passenger since she last rode with him. Holding onto him while he drove had been too personal. It held too many memories. She rode on her own, period.

"You ready?" he asked, firing up the Gold Wing.

She flipped her visor down, tapped her helmet a couple times, and nodded, starting the Harley and letting it rev a bit. He tapped the intercom and shut his bike off.

"What's wrong?"

"I forgot to get pictures!"

"It's ok, don't worry about it."

"Are you kidding? This is Mendocino! Some of the most beautiful real estate in Northern California. These shots will be great. Just give me a minute." He pulled a tripod out of one bag and set the camera on it. "Do you mind a couple of us together?"

"No," she replied. "But we'd better keep the helmets on, so the sunburns don't betray us."

"Good idea. Visors up though," he said, setting the timer. "They'll be far enough away that you won't see the color differences." They took a couple of pictures arm-in-arm and with thumbs up, ocean in the background, and then he took the camera off the tripod and told her to ride the street that paralleled the ocean a few times for some action shots. He adjusted the camera then crossed the road and waited, rapid firing the shutter as she went by.

THEY PULLED into the town of Jenner just as colors were filling the sky. Goat Rock Beach sat on a small peninsula, right where the Russian River comes in off the Pacific.

"I remember this place!" she exclaimed.

"You wanted to see the baby seals."

"Oh, they were so cute!"

"As I recall, you wanted to save them all from death and extinction."

"That does sound like me." She smiled.

"It took me a while to convince you that it was harp seals that were endangered, not harbor seals."

"I'm still a pretty staunch environmentalist." Abby laughed.

Trevor started to take the blanket out of his trunk, stopping momentarily. The reality of what that blanket represented setting in. He hesitated and looked at her, eyebrows up.

She shrugged, not knowing what else to say. The sun was setting fast and they didn't have much time. He pulled it out and they started walking.

They chose a section of beach where there weren't as many people, and Abby settled in between his legs to stay warm. He pulled the blanket around his shoulders and wrapped them both in it together. It was surprising how easily they fell back into their old routine. She leaned her head against his chest, and he kissed her neck. She could tell he was taking in the scent of leather and her hair and the vague remnants of their earlier encounter.

"I want to make love to you again," he whispered in her ear. "I can't get enough of you." Trevor had always been particularly amorous. They triggered one another's passions just by being in the same space.

"I guess you never got over that," she replied, watching the sun begin to dip.

"Got over what?" he murmured, nuzzling into her neck and lighting her fire again.

"Your constant desire for sex." She shivered.

"I don't have a constant desire for sex." He stopped kissing and looked over her shoulder. "What I have is a deep, aching, unrelenting desire for *you*, Abby." He traced a line from her earlobe to her clavicle with soft kisses. "You do something to me that I can't explain in words. I've never been like this with other women."

It was hard, hearing words like that. It sounded like a line, but it was a line she desperately wanted to believe. Not that it would change anything. It just felt better knowing she wasn't the only one who'd been left floating in the void. The sky exploded in hues of blue, green, and orange, and they watched it without saying anything more, in awe of the power and beauty of Mother Earth. They stayed put until the sun was mostly down, then folded up the blanket and got back on the bikes.

It WAS a silent ride the rest of the way home. They didn't use the comms and tried to focus on staying alert as they navigated the dark, curvy roads. Trevor insisted on going first, and she didn't argue. She had enough arguments gnawing at the edges of her mind. By the time they pulled up at Abby's place, it was about nine o'clock. She had given herself permission to enjoy one day with him, and the day wasn't over yet.

"Do you want to come in for a cup of hot tea and thaw out for a bit?" she asked.

"That'd be nice, thanks."

"Don't forget to grab the blanket." She smiled, stowing her gear and locking the saddle bags.

Trevor inhaled as he took the blanket out again and smiled to himself.

"That's disgusting," she pointed out. "I get your smell thing and all, but that's—"

"A memory I'm going to keep for the rest of my life," he replied matter-of-factly.

His comments tended to shut her up. What was she supposed to say to something like that, anyway?

He followed her into the house and immediately took off his shoes and socks. "Do you mind if I use your bathroom?"

"No, go ahead. End of the hallway."

Abby started the tea and turned on the fireplace.

"How many bedrooms do you have?" Trevor wondered, returning from the bathroom.

"Technically three, but I use one as a home office. I know it's a little much for one person, but I wanted to have a guest room." Truth be told, she was hoping she'd find someone, someday, and maybe even leave room for a family.

"I'm hoping to find a place like this for me and Kelsey, just as soon as I get things sorted with the business. Living with my parents isn't exactly my end game."

"I get it. And rentals can be hit or miss. That's why I wanted to buy something and settle with the market." Abby poured their tea and handed him a cup. "Unless you'd prefer a glass of wine?"

He shook his head. "Tea is fine, thanks."

"Maybe you should consider flipping houses. You could do small jobs on the weekends, when you're not working for your dad."

"Yeah. Maybe."

"So many people have lost or damaged property after all the fires the last couple of years. This is a ripe market."

"I know. Why do you think my dad's business needs help? He's got more work than his outfit knows how to handle."

"Something to think about." Abby took a sip of her tea. "I'm going to go throw this blanket in the laundry, before you ask it out on a date."

Trevor shook his head. "Very funny."

"Make yourself comfortable."

Abby started the laundry and decided to brush her teeth and comb out her hair. The sunburn looked ridiculous and the server's peeling comment made her nervous. She used a natural lotion made from olive oil, beeswax, and chamomile, then reapplied deodorant and changed out of her jeans in favor of a pair of lounge pants and an oversized T-shirt. She took a few deep breaths. It had been a long day and she was tired, but her mind wouldn't stop running through the scenes from that afternoon.

She found Trevor sitting by the fire, wiggling his toes and watching the flames. It was strange having a man in her living room since she had never once entertained a guest here. She'd been alone long enough that it felt weird acting like a semi-normal adult; someone who invited a man in and sat by the fire drinking tea. She topped off the hot water in her cup and went to join him, pulling a blanket off the couch along the way.

She spread the blanket out and kneeled down.

"What's that?" He motioned to the small jar in her hand.

"It's a really good natural lotion that will help your face not to peel. Can I put some on you?"

She opened the lid and waved it under his nose. "Smells good."

"We do make quite the pair right about now." She ran her hands through his curls and smoothed the hair back from his face, then carefully rubbed some lotion into his skin. "There. That should help." Abby replaced the lid and leaned on her heels.

"How is it you even look gorgeous in pajamas?" He slid her hair behind her shoulder and let the back of his hand drift down her arm.

She still felt warm on the inside from their earlier encounter and the way he was looking at her wasn't helping. "These aren't my pajamas. I just wanted to be more comfortable. I hate sitting around in jeans."

"Do you mind if I take mine off too?" He reached for the button on his pants but then stopped. "I'm kidding."

The truth was, she didn't mind, but she couldn't say that out loud, so instead she said "Why did you bring your pajamas?"

"I did actually." He started to reach for the button on his jeans again. "I've got them right here." He winked at her and then his face turned serious. "You're amazing. Thank you."

"It's just lotion. You're welcome."

"Not just for that. Thank you." He looked deep into her eyes.

"For what?"

"For giving us this day. For letting go with me."

She rolled off onto one side and pulled the blanket over her legs. "Honestly, I'm a little surprised myself, being the ice queen and all."

Trevor chuckled. "You're not an ice queen, Abby. Far from it. You've just been angry and hurt for a long time, and that's on me. But I need you to know I don't have any expectations going forward. This day has been a gift. And if we never have another one, I'll still be grateful for the experience."

She tried to process the truth of that. The depth of it. "Now what?"

"Well, I guess that depends."

"On?" she asked.

"On whether the day is officially over, or if we've still got a couple of hours before I turn into a pumpkin."

"Oh, so you're the carriage, are you?" Abby smiled knowingly. "And I'm the one wearing the glass slippers?"

"I'm no prince. I know that." He reached over and slipped his hand beneath her hair, cupping her face in one hand. "But I'd like to carry you a little further if you don't mind. Into the night. Into pleasure." He swallowed, searching her eyes. "Will you give me just a little more time?"

She nodded and they kissed. The fire was warm, and he pulled away long enough to get a second blanket to spread underneath them and some pillows from the couch. She watched as he moved confidently, carefully making a soft space for her to land.

"Here. Let's just lay together."

Abby lay down facing the fire, watching the flames, while he turned out the lamp and took off his shirt.

"Permission to put my pajamas on ma'am?"

Her mouth curved into a smile as he removed his jeans and tucked in behind her. He propped himself up on one elbow and played with her hair, then slipped his hand up under her shirt, rubbing the skin in between her breasts.

"When you're down in Argentina," he whispered, kissing her neck. "In the heat of the South American summer, I want you to remember this moment. Remember when you were cold from a long ride through the mountains and you needed the warmth of a fire and a good man to sustain you."

His warmth was inviting, and his touch was so comforting. She snuggled into him and promptly fell asleep.

A couple of hours later, Abby rolled over to find Trevor fast asleep. For a few moments she watched him, wondering what would become of the two of them. She got up to use the bathroom and when she returned, he still hadn't stirred. The light from the fireplace was casting a warm orange glow across his chest.

She took her clothes off before joining him under the blankets and began stroking his skin in the firelight. She followed her fingers with her tongue, causing him to twitch and breathe deeper, coming back to life. Her hair spilled onto his stomach and he began to moan, reaching instinctively for her.

"We fell asleep," he murmured. "Again."

"Mm-hmm," she mumbled, still licking his chest and kissing his stomach.

"Has the clock struck midnight yet?"

"I don't think so." She reached between his legs and

brought the back of her hand slowly over his boxers, turning her fingers just in time to slide over him on the way by.

Trevor sucked in his breath when she touched him. "Thank goodness," he whispered, blinking his eyes awake. He stared at her body, aglow in the firelight, and reached down to stroke one of her breasts.

"Abby, you're so beautiful. I know I can't take real pictures of you like this," he conceded. "That's why I take them in my head. To remember them. To remember you. Right now. Like this."

She pulled away and smiled, kneeling between his legs and carefully removing his boxers.

She bent over him and began using her tongue, drawing her hair over one shoulder to get it out of the way. He watched the flames dance off her skin as she put him in her mouth and brought him to the edge. When she finally mounted him, their bodies fell right back into rhythm, as they rolled and turned in the firelight. It was hours before they came up for air.

WHEN THE LIGHT first started to break through the windows in the kitchen, they were still lying by the fire, stroking one another's skin and alternately kissing and nodding off to sleep.

"I should put you to bed," he murmured.

"No," she protested sleepily. "It's not midnight yet. I checked."

He turned his head in the direction of the windows. "The light betrays you."

She sighed heavily. "Trevor, what are we going to do about this?"

He squeezed her shoulders. "I don't know, Abbs. That's up to you."

"But—"

"No. No buts. You've got three months to go work this out.

More if you need it. If you come back and say, Trevor, that was a one-time thing, I'll accept that. I told you I don't have any expectations. But if there's even a small part of you that might still want me? I'm in. I'm all in."

Abby pushed her face into his chest, trying not to cry. He kissed her forehead, pulling her chin up to look at him.

"I love you, Abby. I loved you then, I love you now, and I will love you for the rest of my life. Whether you return those feelings or not, that's just the way it is. But I'm not stupid. I know how complicated this is, and I respect you enough not to elbow my way in where I'm not wanted. I hope you know that."

She nodded, tears filling her eyes. "Ok."

She didn't have an answer for him. Not at all. And certainly not on the heels of the last twenty-four hours. Nights like that were rare, and she might need all of the next three months just to process the nuances of all that had transpired between the two of them.

"Come on." He sat up, pulling her with him. "Let me tuck you into bed. We both need some sleep."

He wrapped her in one of the blankets and himself in the other and led her down the hall. Turning down the covers, he loaded her in and kneeled next to the bed.

"Lie with me?" she asked. "Until I fall asleep?"

He shook his head, brushing the hair gently away from her face. "I don't think that's a good idea. I'd better get home."

She nodded. He was right, of course, but she didn't want it to end. "Trev?"

"Yeah?"

The words stuck in her throat. She knew better than to push them out at the wrong time, so she just watched him, watching her. "Keep the rubber down."

"I will. I'm sure we'll see you before you go. Kelsey will want to say goodbye."

"Ok."

"Why don't you come by the house for dinner on Tuesday? My parents would love to see you."

"Let's see how badly our faces are peeling by then." She smiled at him.

"If I don't see you...or even if I do, I won't be able to do this." He leaned in for a soft kiss. "Bye, Abbs. Safe travels."

She heard him use the bathroom and gather his things. She even heard him flip the switch on the fireplace and put their cups in the dishwasher. When the door shut behind him, she rolled onto her back and stared at the ceiling.

"What the hell have I done?"

10

Trevor only texted her once on Sunday, to ask if she was ok. She'd slept until noon, and his name was the first thing she saw when she looked at her phone. She replied with a simple *yes* but in reality, her heart was a mess and her body ached for more of him. She spent the rest of the day packing and planning for her trip, trying to keep her mind occupied. She took care of some last-minute details for the Patagonia group and checked in with her accountant.

Frannie worked at the bank with Jake and did Abby's books on the side. For a while she thought maybe Frannie was also doing Jake on the side, but it turned out Frannie's secret relationship was with a guy she'd met at Comic-Con. She felt guilty for doubting Jake's integrity, but it was one of those trigger things that had never gone away.

The inheritance was gone, and this next three months would be the first time she was living explicitly on her earnings from the business. Traveling was easy when there was a big chunk of cash in the bank, but she'd made it last a good long time by living frugally, stretching her dollars and finding ways to cluster expenditures. She'd be ending this next stretch in

Costa Rica, and the cost of living was a bit higher there. Hopefully she'd built a strong enough foundation to carry it all.

The money was never meant to last indefinitely, but somehow knowing it was gone felt a lot like losing her parents all over again. The grief began rolling together and coming in waves. Trevor, her parents, Claire...The collective weight of it all was making the overcast day seem especially gloomy. Grief from her parents' death had given way to acceptance after the first year, but there were still times when it felt like being buried alive. On those days she would go off on a hike or spend a day at the beach. Mountains or waves, it made no difference. Contemplating the distant landscape forced her to look ahead instead of behind. It had a tendency to reset her perspective.

She stared for a while at the picture of her sitting on a bike between the mountains and the ocean, and suddenly her heart couldn't reconcile the truth. The truth was, the connection with Trevor was just as deep and meaningful then as it was now. It wasn't just some silly montage of a memory that belonged in a Redbox rom-com. It was a perfect day, like the one they just had.

After it was over with Trevor, she told herself to just keep moving, but what if simply moving was different from actually moving on? What if she had done one but not the other? A small spark and a little dry fuel and they were on fire all over again. It was arrogant to have thought she could handle it. Turns out the coals were still hot underneath.

HER FACE DID START to peel, but she kept applying lotion several times a day and it seemed to be helping. She figured she could probably put a little makeup on to even out her skin tones. That and a ball cap would just about do the trick.

Kelsey emailed some layout options for the website, which included a couple of the pictures Trevor had taken on Saturday.

She'd told Kelsey during their sit-down at Pop's that it was ok to post pictures and adjust the website, as long as she ran them through Abby first for permission. This was her asking permission.

The photos were excellent. It must have taken Trevor the better part of the day to edit them. He just kept on surprising her. Seeing the photos only made the spinning worse. There was no way to mix logic and emotion in the right proportions. They just swirled together in a bitter cocktail of unpalatable choices.

On Monday afternoon, Lauren called.

"Hey, stranger! Where have you been?"

"Just getting ready for my trip."

"Well, the girls are asking about you. Don't you leave on Wednesday?"

"Wednesday. Yes."

"Well, come over for dinner tonight then, would you?"

"Sure—yeah."

"What's wrong?"

"Nothing. I'm just distracted right now. I'm prepping for three more months on the road." She hated being cagey with Lauren, but this twenty-four-hour rendezvous with Trevor was a lot to throw out there, and she really didn't want to get into it on the phone. "I'll talk to you when I get there."

"Ok. Be here around five. Jake will get home with the girls about six, and that'll give us time to catch up while they're at soccer practice."

"Sounds good."

When she got to the house, Lauren nearly pulled her arm out of its socket yanking her through the door for a hug.

"Come here, you. I can't believe you're leaving me again! When are you going to actually stick around for a while?"

"It smells great in here." Abby remarked. "Which candle is that?"

"Clean linen, I think."

Clean linen fit perfectly. Lauren's house was always clean and tidy, a feat that seemed impossible to Abby with two kids running around all the time. She had them on specific schedules that were posted on the fridge with activities and homework and time built in for play. It was an impressive bit of organizational magic. Similar, in fact, to the way she organized her tours. Maybe they were more alike than Abby realized.

She shrugged out of her leather jacket and hung it on a hook in the foyer, then slipped her feet out of her boots. "After this, I'll be home for a couple months before the next one, I promise. It makes more sense to squish tours together if I can. It costs less in airfare, and I can rent the same bike for three months straight—which is way cheaper."

A couple of months here. With Trevor. And Kelsey. And a whole hell of a lot of question marks that she hoped to find answers for.

"You want some wine?" Lauren offered.

Abby looked outside at her bike and then looked at the clock. "Ok. I can probably have one glass."

She was extremely strict about drinking and riding, and she would only have a beer or glass of wine if she was at least an hour from getting back on the bike. This was something she never compromised on during the tours either. It was clearly spelled out in the waivers signed by each participant. They agreed not to drink and ride and to abide by the rule or risk being sent home early. She had seen too much. Horrific accidents had happened right in front of her with people who were stone cold sober. Riding was already a risk, and the liability wasn't worth it.

It was harsh, but necessary. Abby spent a good long time at the beginning of each tour explaining her reasons and the one-and-done consequences of violating the agreement, so that everyone knew exactly what they were agreeing to. So far, she hadn't had to send anyone home, but she did have to take someone's keys once. That was about as much grace as she had.

At the end of each day, when they were done riding and settled into whatever their lodging option might be for the night, they could drink all they wanted, just not during the day. If they wanted to get on the bikes the next morning with a hangover, that was their business.

"Dinner is already in the oven. I made a roast, so we have time to relax. Let's go to the living room." Lauren handed her a glass of wine. "I'm so proud of you Abbs. I feel like my life is so boring compared to yours."

"Are you kidding me?" Abby walked through the house noticing what a warm and inviting space it was, compared to the relatively sterile environment of the condo. "Have you *seen* the schedule on your fridge? You're way busier than I am. Besides, you're raising humans! I am so not equipped to do that."

"Of course you are," Lauren replied. "You're just living your dreams right now."

"So are you. You've wanted this since you were a little girl. I'm the one who got stuck playing Barbies with you, remember? I'm pretty sure the dream house was decorated identically to this one." Abby spun in a circle, gesturing around the room. She ended her spin by sitting on the couch, a gutsy move for someone holding red wine over off-white fabric.

"Ok, yes. I did want to be a mom and have a house. But I've never really been anywhere." Her voice got quieter. "Sometimes my life feels small compared to yours."

Where was this coming from? Lauren had never mentioned

anything like this before. "Are you having an early mid-life crisis?" Abby wondered. "Is everything ok with Jake?"

"Fine, yeah. I just—sometimes I really envy you with your jet-setting lifestyle."

"It's not that glamorous, believe me. Before I got home, I hadn't had a proper shower in weeks. I sleep in a lot of seedy hotels and I've eaten things that would make you cringe." Abby leaned forward. "Look what you've built here, Lauren. You've built a life. A family. A community. A comfortable home. I love coming here because your house always feels warm and—I don't know, *lived in*."

"Well your place would feel lived in too if you actually *lived* there," Lauren replied, sitting in a cushioned, overstuffed chair next to her. She pulled a soft blanket down and covered her legs.

"Touché." Abby raised her glass.

"Do you still think about having kids?" Lauren asked. "Did you think about it with Eric?"

"I did, but we never talked about it." This was a tricky question. She hadn't thought about it in a long time. "I don't think nomads and chefs make for very good parents."

"You don't have to be a nomad, you know."

"Yes, but what would I *do* around here, Lauren? I've worked odd jobs, done a few things I enjoyed, but nothing has ever lit my fire like this. I love traveling. I love going new places and meeting people from all over the world. I love learning languages and exploring strange foods. And I love the people I get to work with. I feel like I was made for this, and it doesn't jive too well with families and stability."

"I know, and I can see that you're happy in your work, but I also know there's something missing. At least with Eric you had the freedom to travel and he was happy to let you be you."

It was true. Eric didn't try to hold her down like most guys would. Still, being gone for months at a time was a challenge for any relationship. Even the one with her sister.

For Abby, being gone meant experiencing growth and diversity. Coming back felt unusually stagnant. The town was the same. Lauren and Jake were the same. Their kids were growing and changing, and they were great, but it still felt like extra work trying to reconnect and keep their relationship strong. That was the blessing and the curse of time and distance.

"I need to ask you something."

"This sounds serious." Lauren looked concerned. "Are you ok?"

"Maybe. Maybe not." She took a sip of her wine. "Back when all the shit went down with Trevor, did he ever write me letters? Maybe letters that Mom kept from me?"

The look of shock on Lauren's face told the truth before the words left her mouth. "Not that I know of, why? What's this about?" She held a hand in front of her face. "Wait. Back up. What the hell is going on with you and Trevor?"

"What about Aunt Jane? Do you think she would have kept letters from me?"

"Abby! Fess up! What the fuck?"

"Calm down. I'm getting to it."

Lauren took a large gulp of wine, nearly finishing the glass. "Hold that thought. I'm getting the bottle, and I don't care if you have to spend the night." She poured them both more wine, even though Abby had barely touched hers. "The last I knew, you saw him at Pop's and gave Kelsey a ride back to his folks' place. You saw him again?"

Abby held up two fingers.

"Twice? That was just last week! When were you going to tell me?"

"He came over that night after I dropped Kelsey off and brought me a new helmet—to replace the one she broke.

Which totally wasn't necessary, of course. Anyway, we talked, and there may have been...a kiss." Heat crept into Abby's neck as she shrugged one shoulder.

"Ok. This is definitely getting interesting. By the way, what's going on with your face? Is that a sunburn?"

"We went riding on Saturday."

"You and Kelsey?"

"Me and Trevor. Trevor and I," she corrected herself.

Lauren's eyebrows raised as she tapped a finger against her lips. "Um. Last time I checked, you wear a full-face helmet with a sun visor." She tipped her head sideways, studying Abby's complexion. "How did you get sunburned on just half your face?"

"Pretty sure it was from falling asleep in the sun." One heartbeat. Two. "After having sex."

Lauren leaned forward, nearly spitting out her wine. "Shut the fuck up! You did not!"

"We did."

"Oh, thank God!"

Abby did a double take. "Hey! Whose side are you on, anyway?"

Lauren smirked as if the question was ridiculous. "You're my sister and I want what's best for you, but I've always been team Trevor and you know it."

"You think Trevor is what's best for me? That's it. I'm leaving." Abby started to stand.

"Sit your ass down! You're not leaving without giving me full details. Besides, I wasn't a fan of Trevor *then* in particular, of course not. But in general? I've never seen you dialed into anyone the way you were with him. I've never seen your face that bright, your smile so wide."

"I don't even know how to respond to that, Lauren. I mean, seriously? He *fucked* my best friend. Not only that, he got her pregnant. And chose *her* over me. What was I supposed to do?" Reminding herself of all the reasons she should be mad at him stoked the fire of self-righteous indignation.

"To be fair, Abbs, you didn't know about the baby or any of his choices until, like, now. Yes, he walked away, but you didn't give him much choice. It's not like it was premeditated. He didn't even remember doing it."

"So. He. *Said*. God, I can't believe you! My own flesh and blood! You didn't think it was super convenient for him to just *pretend* he blacked out?"

"He had a lot of total blackouts back then. It wasn't an uncommon occurrence," Lauren replied, putting her palm up again. "I'm just saying."

"I guess his sexual indiscretion was the least of my worries," Abby spat. "I guess I shouldn't have been dating someone in a regular habit of being blackout drunk."

"You're right," Lauren conceded. "Can I just say, though, that when he was sober, you two were the best thing that had ever happened to one another? I know how much you loved him Abby. I guess that's what I get sad about. The *could have beens*."

"Yeah, well, welcome to the club!" Abby downed her wine. Lauren picked up the bottle, but she refused. "I'm just going let this go to my head for a while, thanks."

"I'm sorry."

"Ok."

They fought like typical siblings, but they also forgave quickly, which Abby was thankful for. She proceeded to tell Lauren about the ride and the hilltop sex and the opposite-side sunburns.

"Trevor is worse off than me. The whole right side of his body is burned—face, shoulder, arm, leg. Luckily his dick was covered. I have to admit, it's kind of hilarious."

The memory of Trevor standing there naked, looking like

two sides of a coin, was just too funny in hindsight. Abby started laughing. Lauren started laughing.

Soon they were both laughing so hard Lauren began to snort. "That is the funniest damn thing I've ever heard. Did you get pictures?"

"No. We did not get pictures." *Except for those few at the end. At sunset.* They weren't in the batch Kelsey sent, and she was afraid to ask for them. Afraid of what a request like that would mean to him. Or what it might mean to her.

"Could you be serious for a minute?" Abby scolded.

Lauren was still shaking her head and laughing quietly. It took her a few minutes to compose herself. "Ok. Sorry. I'm fine now. Then what happened?"

"We had a late lunch in Mendocino, drove down Highway 1 and stopped to watch the sunset at Goat Rock."

"Goat Rock! Nice!"

"We got to my place about nine. It was a cold ride back in the dark, so I invited him in for a cup of hot tea."

"A cup of tea?" Lauren repeated sarcastically. "Come on. Spill it." She flipped her palm up and waved her fingers inward. "What time did he leave?"

Abby shrugged. "I don't know—about five, I guess."

"Five *a.m.*?"

"Yeah."

"Please tell me you slept most of that time." The look on Lauren's face was sarcastic, as if she already knew the answer.

When Abby shook her head, Lauren's jaw dropped open and her eyes lit up. Then, just as quickly, her face was serious again.

"Abbs, this is a *big* deal. You didn't just have a throw-down on a hilltop. You let it keep going. You let him spend the night."

"I know. I know! But I made a conscious decision early in the day that I wasn't going to talk myself out of it. I was just going to let it play out and see where it went. I knew I was going away, and part of me just wanted one good day to take with me. So, I let go."

"You sure did." Lauren finished her wine and poured another glass.

"Take it easy. Jake's going to wonder what the hell I did to you, getting you drunk before dinner."

"Are you kidding? Jake's gonna be one happy man after I put the girls to bed. Just thinking about your free-love hilltop escapades and marathon sex sessions has me thinking it's been way too long for this girl!"

"Don't tell Jake about the sex. Please? I'm pretty sure they still talk, and I don't want Trevor knowing I told you guys. Promise me, Lauren!"

"All right! Geez!"

They sat for a while, listening to the clock ticking in the hallway.

Lauren's voice softened. "I never saw any letters. I'm sorry. Maybe Aunt Jane knows?"

"Yeah. Maybe."

"How do you feel, Abbs? I mean, really. What do you want?"

It took a minute for the words to form. "I don't know. He's so different now. He's the same sexy, charming bad boy I fell in love with, but all grown up and taking responsibility for his life and his daughter. And I gotta tell you—I may have been a sucker for a bad boy when we were younger...But there's nothing sexier than a badass man who also happens to have his shit together. Did you know he has an MBA?"

"No kidding? Wow." Lauren nodded her approval. "And I'm assuming, based on the all-nighter, he's still an amazing lover?"

Abby tipped her head back against the couch cushion. "I don't know how it's possible, but he's even better than before. He totally puts me first, you know? Makes sure I'm taken care of. It was like being under some kind of a spell!"

Lauren started fanning herself with a magazine. "Jake is *definitely* getting a piece of this tonight."

Abby laughed. "It's not like I planned for this to happen. But now I have no *fucking* clue what to do about it. Pardon the pun."

"Well, it's a good thing you've got three months to figure shit out."

"I know, right?"

"I'm proud of you for letting go. I'm just worried about that heart of yours." Lauren pointed her finger at Abby's chest.

Just then the door opened and the girls came bounding in, tackling Abby and almost spilling her wine. She set it on the end table and gave them both a huge hug.

"Hey, short stops! How was practice?"

Lauren's youngest, Emily crossed her arms, jutting one hip out to the side. She had just turned eight, and was an expert on every subject.

"We play *soccer*, not baseball Aunt Abby!"

"My mistake." Abby tipped her head up toward the ceiling. "You guys are wide receivers, right?"

"That's *football!*" Becca yelled, giggling.

"You sure tackle like football players!" She started tickling them and they screamed and wiggled free. Abby looked over her shoulder and watched Lauren walk by Jake and kiss him on the cheek, pinching his ass.

"Dinner's almost ready," she called out without looking back.

Jake's eyebrows lifted and he looked at Lauren, then over at Abby. "Bedtime, girls! Nice seeing you, Abby!"

"Bedtime! Dad, we haven't had dinner yet!" Emily whined.

Abby just laughed. For all his smart-ass commentary, Jake was perfect for Lauren and she was happy for her sister. They'd built a life and a family that worked for them.

Abby had always been a dreamer with a heavy sprinkling of

wanderlust. Besides, at thirty-six years old, it was getting to the point where having children might not be a physical reality. Her tour groups filled that void, for the most part. She was no Brené Brown, but her degree in psychology definitely wasn't going to waste. She tried to advise and challenge them in ways that were both intentional and authentic, as if she were a mother hen to her little groups of biker chicks.

Three years earlier she had started with a thirst for adventure, but quickly realized what she was searching for was her own truth. This method of traveling with intention was something she picked up in a book called *The Art of Pilgrimage*. She read it in India on a very spiritual part of her journey, and the concepts stuck. She started journaling and seeking out signposts of wisdom. All along the way she encountered people and situations that helped move her further along her path.

Of course, you're always the last person to notice faults in yourself. Seeing Trevor again made it abundantly clear that she hadn't come as far as she thought.

At dinner, the girls chattered about school and soccer, and Lauren kept filling Jake's wine glass. Abby asked Jake about work and they caught up on some of the problems facing the town as it grew and expanded into a destination for wineries and spa getaways. Jake's work at the bank kept his finger on the pulse of the business community. He was also a wannabe politician who sat on the city council and helped make important decisions about the future of Calistoga.

Lauren served fruit for dessert in fancy glasses layered with some sort of chia seed and almond milk pudding and the girls devoured it. Abby loved Lauren's cooking, and missed it when she was on the road.

"Ok, the big people get the dishes. I'm going to do bath time with these soccer queens!" Abby announced. "It is soccer, right? Not baseball?"

"Yes! Soccer! That's what we've been talking about this

whole time!" Emily's voice was exaggerated and high pitched and her missing teeth made her all the more adorable when she got excited.

"Yay!" The girls yelled and pushed away from the table.

"Go run the tub. I'll be right up!"

"I got you!" Becca pointed at Abby. Being the older sister, she felt very much in charge of Emily's bedtime routine. Abby would just be along for the ride.

"Thanks, Abby." Jake smiled.

"My pleasure. After all, I'm not going to see the little squirts until spring!"

"I can't believe you're missing Christmas. *Again!*" Lauren complained.

"I'll send gifts for the girls from Brazil. And we'll video chat!"

"Next year, can we please have your actual face?"

"I'll think about it." Abby's head tilted left and right. "Now, you two behave yourselves. I'll send the girls down for kisses before bed."

As she was heading up the stairs, she heard Jake saying, "Seriously, Lauren. What's gotten into you? Not that I'm complaining or anything..." Their voices faded as she reached the top of the stairs and was attacked by naked little girls careening toward the bathroom. Abby walked along picking up pieces of clothing and deposited them in the hamper before opening the bathroom door. "Who's ready for some splashing?"

Squeals of delight filled the house as the next hour was spent bathing and combing out the girls' hair, then sending them downstairs to say goodnight. She read them a bedtime story, tucked them into their twin beds with the pink duvet covers, and kissed them both goodbye.

"Aunt Abby, are you an explorer?" Becca wanted to know.

"Why do you ask?" Abby knelt down and smoothed Becca's hair.

"We've been studying explorers like Lewis and Clark in school. They discovered new places and traveled to lots of places where people hadn't been before. Is that what you do? I told my teacher Mrs. Stevens that my aunt was an explorer," she finished proudly.

"I am an explorer in one sense," Abby explained. "An explorer is an adventurer and I definitely go on a lot of adventures. But I'm not discovering new lands. Everywhere I ride my motorcycle has already been discovered. Does that make sense?"

Becca nodded. "You're still my favorite explorer! I like following you on the map with my mom."

Abby kissed her forehead. "I'm glad! You can send me messages too."

"When I grow up I want to be an explorer too!"

"You would make a great explorer."

WHEN SHE GOT DOWNSTAIRS, she found Lauren and Jake making out in the kitchen. "Hey, lovebirds! I'm leaving." She pulled on her boots as Lauren hurried over.

"Oh, Abbs! Have a great trip and keep in contact, ok? You know how I worry about you."

"I'll send you updates and messages like always—and you and the girls can track me on the maps."

"I know. It's just...if anything happens, you're so far away." It was the same conversation they always had when Abby was leaving. Jake put his arm around Lauren and gave her a squeeze.

"It's going to be fine, Lauren. I'm going to be fine," Abby said soothingly.

11

Ever since their parents died, Lauren had been on-edge about Abby's travels. Maybe that was why she was all upside down and asking Abby about having kids. It had been a while since they had a conversation like that. Losing both of their parents so suddenly had been exceptionally difficult for each of them in their own way. Emotions and grief tended to seep out sideways sometimes, even so long after the fact.

It was a car accident that killed them, but they still didn't know for sure what happened. Their father pretty much chain-smoked and never took care of his diabetes. The best they could figure from the autopsy was that he had a stroke while driving and ended up killing them both.

Lauren had been close with their mother. Abby was more of a daddy's girl. Growing up, she'd loved hanging out with him in the garage while he was fixing cars. When she met Trevor, it wasn't a big leap for him to teach her about the smaller and simpler engine of a motorcycle. Her father never made her feel like a tomboy for liking cars and engines. Although he wasn't Trevor's biggest fan, it was more because he never considered anyone good enough for her.

After Abby bought her own bike, her dad took over where Trevor left off, and together they learned how to take apart and rebuild her first project bike. They would talk for hours about life and all the places Abby wanted to see. Pete had been a mechanic in the navy and told stories about traveling with the Pacific Fleet to ports of call from Asia to Australia.

He never traveled after that, mostly because Abby was born a few months after he separated from the service, but he would get a faraway look in his eye when he remembered the people and landscapes of the countries he'd visited.

He made Abby promise she would visit those countries someday too, so after he died, Asia was the first continent she selected. She then spent the better part of a year traveling from Japan to New Zealand, with several smaller islands thrown in as well. That first year just about killed Lauren.

Abby tried to check in often, but cell service was sketchy, and it was a pain trying to buy new prepaid phones in every country she visited. She was often so far from cities and cell towers, there was no way to make a call even if she did stop for a few days at a time. After several months, Lauren mailed her an orange-and-black contraption that looked like an old-school Blackberry with a basic keyboard.

"It's called a SPOT. It's a tracker," she announced when they finally connected by phone. "Every day, you push a button and it will send me a message that you're ok. That's all I ask. I need to know you're alive. The directions are in the box."

Nowadays, Abby never rode in foreign countries without the SPOT strapped to her jacket. It had the added benefit of being able to summon help in an emergency using a satellite location link, and that had come in handy a few times when she was alone.

Once she came upon an accident in Turkey where the driver of the vehicle was badly hurt. They were in the middle of nowhere, and she was able to request help despite the language barrier. She stayed with them until help arrived and the helicopter pilot, who spoke a little English, told her she had saved the man's life.

Thankfully, she never had to use it for any of her riders on a tour. The device had a yearly subscription fee, but between Lauren and the business, it paid for itself several times over in peace of mind.

SHE LEFT Lauren's house and got on the bike, feeling somewhat guilty for missing holidays and birthdays. The girls would only be little once, and she often wondered if being on the road all the time was somehow selfish, but in the end, it was her life to live and no one else's.

On her way home, she thought about Trevor and how he was tied to Kelsey now in a way he hadn't been before. He said that he wasn't always in the picture, as Kelsey was growing up, but with Claire gone, he must be adjusting to a whole new paradigm.

People thought it was brave of her to run her own business on a global scale, but what she did was nothing compared to the business of parenting. Abby had watched Lauren as she became a mother and was in the delivery room when both girls were born. She helped out when she was in town and used to babysit with Eric every couple of weeks so they could have a date night. Eric would make gourmet kid food and they would all watch Disney movies.

It was hard work, raising kids, and Abby had been thankful a thousand times over that she never had to deal with an unexpected pregnancy. She wondered what it would have been like if it had been her instead of Claire who had turned up pregnant? Her life would be completely different.

Almost on cue, as soon as she parked the bike and shut off her engine, a call came in from Trevor. She sat straddling the bike and pressed the button on her headset.

"Hey. What's up?"

He was quiet for a moment, as if he'd forgotten why he called. "Um. Kelsey asked about you tonight. She said she emailed you some ideas and you never responded. I was wondering if you're ok."

"Oh, shoot! Yeah. Tell her I'm sorry. I was at Lauren's all evening. I'll get back to her soon."

"Why don't you tell her yourself?"

"What? When?"

"My parents still want you to come over for dinner. Before you leave."

"How's your face?" She smiled into her helmet, staring at her gauges and absently rubbing the chrome.

"It's not bad, actually. I told you it would turn to a tan pretty quickly. You?"

"I've been putting that lotion on it. I even wore makeup today, but Lauren still noticed."

"Lauren has eyes like a hawk. You can't go by that."

"It's not that bad, I guess. I'm wearing a ball cap everywhere I go."

Trevor laughed. "What do you say? Dinner tomorrow night? I'm pretty sure Mama's making lasagna."

"Oh, now you're just playing dirty."

"Scout's honor."

Abby sighed. "I don't know, Trev."

"Listen, we had our perfect day, and we agreed to leave the fairy tale alone with no expectations after midnight." He cleared his throat. "Ok, so we were a little late on our curfew, but still. I told you no pressure and I meant it. We can be friends, right? If Kelsey is going to work for you, we're going to see each other from time to time."

Abby swallowed the truth of that. It had been rolling around in her mouth for days. It wasn't going to get any easier from here. "Thank you, by the way, for those beautiful photos. When Kelsey sent me the mock-ups, I was really impressed. Pretty sure you missed your calling there."

"The light was good—we got lucky." His voice got quiet.

"How did the other ones turn out?"

"Is that Abby?" She heard Kelsey's voice in the background. "Tell her she *has* to come to dinner! I need to show her what I found out about drivers ed."

"Did you hear that?" He made his voice sound insistent like a teenage girl's. "You *have* to come to dinner."

Abby laughed. For all his faults, he was trying to be a good dad, and she respected that.

"All right. Fine. But I need to make it an early night. I have to get down to SFO for a morning flight."

"Do you need a ride to the airport?"

"No." She tried to hide her annoyance. "I've got it all worked out."

"Ok." An awkward pause ensued. "Um. Dinner is at six tomorrow. I guess we'll see you then?"

"Yeah. See you then."

THE ENTIRE NEXT day was spent on laundry and repacking. She had a system, never carrying more than she could pack onto her bike.

There was a fair amount of minimalism that went into solo motorcycle travel, but electronics were always the issue. Her small laptop and a solar charging system were the two luxuries she couldn't do without. She mostly used her phone or GoPro as cameras but brought a small collapsible tripod for perspective and group shots.

It was the clothing and personal care products where she skimped the most. She generally brought two sets of clothes and three pairs of socks. She always brought a bathing suit and flip-flops, a small travel towel, and one very simple summer dress for special occasions, like when she actually got a shower.

Other than that she brought a ball cap, a small brush and hair ties, deodorant, a toothbrush, lip balm, sunscreen, and a well-stocked first aid kit. It added up quick. Other items could always be bought in country as needed, once she figured out what kind of bike she'd be riding and how much storage it had.

Everything, including her helmet, fit into a duffel small enough for the overhead and a backpack that fit under her seat. Her contact in each country received a shipment ahead of time with a small welcome gift for each participant and the banner for group photos.

When every last detail was taken care of, she showered and blew her hair out and fashioned it into a loose ponytail at the base of her neck. She slathered her body with lotion, paying special attention to her face, and did her best to fix the sunburn with a full coating of foundation and blush on the opposite cheek to even things out a bit. A bit of eye makeup and some lipstick helped draw attention away from the obvious.

Even with all of that, it was still pretty noticeable. It had nothing to do with Lauren's hawklike eyesight. She couldn't wait to be on the ground in Chile, getting on a bike, and becoming invisible for a while.

Trevor's parents were casual people, and dinners at their house were served family style and loud. She set her stuff by the door, pulled on her boots and jacket and grabbed her ball cap off the hook. With any luck, they wouldn't ask her to remove it at dinner.

Here goes nothing. She patted the tank lovingly as she mounted her Harley. "I'm gonna miss you, girl. But don't worry, I'll be back."

She arrived about ten minutes early. Kelsey came running out, carrying a helmet.

"Grandma says dinner won't be ready for another half an hour, because the lasagna has to sit or something. Can we go for a quick ride?"

"I don't know." She looked around. "What does your dad have to say about that?"

"I told her it was fine with me if it was ok with you."

Abby could see Trevor's silhouette inside the screen door, but he was mostly in shadow. She turned her attention back to Kelsey. "Where'd you get that helmet? That's not the one from the garbage, is it?"

"No! My dad bought it for me so I wouldn't have to use your extra one—*and* so that I'll have one when I start training for my learner's permit." She was grinning from ear to ear.

"Let me see that." Abby smiled, turning it around in her hands. "It's very nice! This is a very good brand!"

"I know! He made me do the research on the safety features of each brand, and then we went to the store together and tried on a bunch of helmets until we found one that fit my head the right way."

She glanced toward Trevor, curious about the man in the shadows. Where did he get the money to buy Kelsey a high-end helmet *and* replace Abby's extra, all while living with his parents and supposedly trying to get their own place? She still knew so little about where he'd been and what he'd been doing all these years. She assumed he would stay in Calistoga until Kelsey finished high school, but in reality she had no idea how long he was planning to stick around.

"Ok. Let's see you put it on and buckle it."

Kelsey did as she was told while Abby checked the fit and asked her some questions, which Kelsey knew all the answers to.

"All right then." She popped the visor down for her. "Let's ride!"

She took Kelsey out on a similar route to the one they had taken before, along back roads lined with trees and the smell of fresh pine. When they pulled into the driveway and parked the bike this time, Kelsey made a show of taking her helmet off very carefully and then holding it under her arm. "Thanks, Abby! That was fantastic! Can I get a picture with you to show my friend at school? He thinks I'm kidding that I'm going to learn to ride a motorcycle."

"Oh, *he* does, does he?" She looked over at the porch and there was Trevor again, waiting behind the screen. She could see him shaking his head. "Well, we'll show him!" Abby exclaimed. "Why don't you get on the bike and we'll take the picture like that, ok?"

"Really? Ok." With Abby's help, Kelsey got on and stood next to her while she snapped the picture on her phone. "I'll send it to you. That way you won't forget about me while you're on your trip."

"Like I could ever forget about you." Abby tousled her hair. "You're my virtual assistant. We'll be talking all the time."

By this time, Trevor was standing on the porch staring at Abby. Clearly the two of them wouldn't be talking all the time while she was gone, and it was already awkward, acknowledging that fact. Morning couldn't come soon enough.

"Hey, half-pint, it's lasagna time," he called.

"Yes!" Kelsey made a fist and brought it in toward her ribs. "I love lasagna."

She ran into the house, planting a quick kiss on Trevor's cheek on the way.

"Half-pint? As in *Little House on the Prairie*?" Abby pulled her helmet off and shook out her hair, then pulled it through the ball cap.

"When she was little, I would have her over to my apartment in Tampa. I didn't have cable—just an old TV with an old-school, rabbit-ear antenna—you know the type?" He made a peace sign behind his head for effect.

"I'm familiar with the technology, yes." She reached into her saddle bag and pulled out a bottle of red wine. Calistoga was wine country. About as plentiful as water, it flowed just as freely. No one came to dinner without a bottle in tow. She thought about her one-drink per hour rule and wondered if she could risk the refusal and get out quickly on the early-morning-departure excuse.

Trevor waited until he had her attention again. "We used to eat popcorn and watch *Little House on The Prairie* reruns, because it was one of the only things that came in clear enough to see." He wasn't ashamed. Just telling it like it was.

It wasn't hard to imagine him in a dingy apartment, having picked up an old TV and some rabbit ears at a pawn shop, trying to provide some sense of normalcy for visitations with his daughter. That seemed to fit the no-frills Trevor she remembered. But this Trevor? The one with an MBA and money to spend on six-hundred-dollar helmets? She wasn't sure she knew *him* at all.

HE HELD the door so she could enter the house and she was immediately assaulted by his mother's exuberance.

"Abby! It's so good to see you, dear." Trevor's mother was a hugger, just like Gil. She was a large Italian woman with ample breasts that always made Abby feel like she was suffocating.

"Renee. It's good to see you too. Thanks for having me over. You know how I love your Italian food!"

"Let me see your lovely face!" The older woman took Abby's

hat off without permission. That was just the way Renee operated.

She looked at Abby and smiled, grabbing her face in both of her chubby hands and kissing her soundly on one cheek. It was all Abby could do not to grimace as her hands pulled on the sensitive skin on the sunburned side. Then, she put Abby at arm's length and turned her chin from side to side. She looked over at Trevor and smiled, shaking her head with her breasts jiggling as she laughed quietly.

"You can put it back on, dear." She handed the hat to Abby with a knowing smile.

Thankfully, neither Gil nor Kelsey had been the wiser, although his dad did make a crack about how Trevor had fallen asleep with one arm in the shade and the other in the sun. Obviously, they hadn't seen the rest of his body.

Trevor was lucky. Although his father's Irish side made him appear pale, his dark curls and ability to tan came from his mother. His skin was almost back to normal, although one side did look a little browner than the other at the moment.

They grilled Abby with fifteen years' worth of questions, to the point where she did take them up on a second glass of wine. She knew by then that getting out quickly was not an option.

If dying from embarrassment was on the menu, she might have chosen that over sitting through the next two hours of a multi-course Italian meal with those meaningful looks that his mother kept giving the two of them.

She fed them and fed them until Abby was so stuffed, she wanted to unbutton her jeans. She engaged Kelsey in a discussion about her drivers ed course and promised to start their riding lessons when she got back.

"So, tell us about this next trip." Trevor asked, though he knew the answers full well.

Abby turned her attention to Gil and Renee. "I'm doing a

route through northern Patagonia that includes the Chilean and Argentinian sides of the Andes, then doing a tour in Brazil, and another in Costa Rica before returning to the States in early spring."

"Are you going through the countries in alphabetical order?" Kelsey asked.

"What? No!" Abby laughed. "I mean—well, I guess it does appear that way this go-round. I never really thought about it that way."

"We could do a poll!"

"What?"

"On the website!" Kelsey's face lit up. "We could talk about the ABCs of travel and ask people to vote on the next tour—ok, like, list a bunch of countries that start with D and people could vote—you know, like those *Choose Your Own Adventure* books my mom used to read to me."

At the mention of her mom, Kelsey's face fell and she looked for a moment like she might cry.

"Well, let's brainstorm!" Abby jumped on the bandwagon for Kelsey's sake. "Who can think of a country that starts with D?" She looked around the table, eyes pleading.

"Denmark!" Trevor announced.

"Dominican Republic!" Gil chimed in.

Kelsey looked up. "Forget it. It's a dumb idea."

"It's not a dumb idea!" Abby corrected. "Let's keep going. Countries that begin with E?"

"Ethiopia," Renee offered.

"Estonia," Gil added.

"Egypt!" Kelsey yelped, then stuck her hand over her mouth. "Sorry. That was extra."

"How about Ecuador?" Abby said.

"El Salvador," Trevor finished. "And speaking of geography, don't you have social studies homework?" He directed his attention to Kelsey.

"Oops."

"Why don't you *oops* yourself upstairs and work on that? I'll let you know when Abby's leaving so you can come say goodbye."

"Ok." Kelsey looked at Abby as she picked up her plate and excused herself from the table. "The ABCs. Think about it!"

"I will. I promise. The idea's growing on me. There are a lot of fun marketing angles we could take with that."

After Kelsey went upstairs, Renee offered her more wine. "No, thank you. I have to ride. The lasagna was delicious. Thank you so much."

"If you think you're leaving, missy, you've got another thing coming!" A voice called from the back door.

"Isabella? Oh, my god!" Abby nearly jumped out of her chair, elated to hear the voice of Trevor's sister. The two women embraced. "It's so good to see you. I didn't know you were back here too."

"I'm not," she said, taking off her coat and sitting down in the seat Kelsey had vacated. "I live in the city now, but when I heard the ghost of Abby Steel was making a rare appearance at the family table, I just had to come and see for myself."

Abby shook her head. "God, Izzy, it's been ages! What are you up to?"

"Isabella, what? Your mother doesn't get a kiss?" Renee stretched out her arms and waited until Izzy stood up.

"Sorry, Mama." She gave her mother a kiss on the cheek and bent over for a hug. "How are you?"

"Good, good, now go get yourself a plate and eat something while you talk. Trevor, get the wine."

Trevor poured some wine into a fresh glass, but he was staring at Abby.

Isabella walked into the dining room and stopped, wagging her pointer finger back and forth. "What's going on between you two?"

Abby looked at Trevor, but he had already looked away. "What? Nothing."

"Bullshit."

"Isabella!" her mother scolded.

"Sorry, Mama."

Abby decided to fill the silence while Izzy filled her plate. "I'm leaving for Chile and Argentina tomorrow."

"Quit changing the subject." Izzy stared across the table.

Isabella had always been wildly outspoken. This was a trait Abby admired, but there was no fucking way this conversation was going down in front of Trevor's parents, and Abby needed to make that perfectly, indisputably clear. Abby just kept on talking, completely ignoring her. "After that it's Brazil and then Costa Rica."

Izzy forked some lasagna into her mouth. "One of my colleagues is from one of the beach towns in Costa Rica. I can't remember the name of it, but anyway—she's moving back in January, for a few months. I should connect you two!"

"Does she ride a motorcycle?"

"No, but her brother does, and he is one *fine* specimen of a man, let me tell you. I've seen pictures. Maybe she would introduce you." Izzy glanced over at Trevor, whose face was unchanged, but he tightened the grip on his fork. "I'll send you her contact info. She's really sweet. I think she shares the beach house with her brother. Maybe you could crash there if you need some down time." Izzy said the words *down time* as if they were code for getting laid by a hot Costa Rican man.

"Sure," Abby replied with a smile. "I always like to make solid contacts in country."

Trevor took a sip of his wine and stared straight ahead, showing no reaction whatsoever.

Izzy pulled out her phone and tapped around a few times. She handed her phone across the table, but Renee scolded her.

"Isabella! No phones at the table!"

"I'm just getting her number, Mama! So we can keep in touch. Type your number in for me, would you?"

Abby took the phone but instead of a contact card there was a picture of a very good-looking man on a motorcycle parked next to a beach. She looked at Izzy, who raised her thick black eyebrows but feigned ignorance. "Oh, I'm sorry. Is that the wrong screen? Here, give it to me."

Abby handed the phone back, but not before Trevor got a glance of what they were looking at. "What are you, twelve?" He said to his sister, not even trying to hide the irritation in his voice.

"You stay out of this. It's just girl talk!"

Abby, who typed in her contact info, and the tension died down as Izzy fired a barrage of legitimate questions across the table. She and Abby then entered into an animated conversation about all things travel and work. For the next forty-five minutes, Abby talked all about riding solo in foreign countries, and what the culture was like in this country or that, and what she *actually* did in her *down time*, which was a whole lot of sleeping and eating and planning and research. Trevor sat listening intently as Abby told story after story of comical and downright terrifying things that had happened to her along the way.

"Come on, Renee, I'll help you with the dishes. Let's leave these kids alone," Gil announced, turning his attention to Abby. "Now, sugar plum, you make sure and give old Gil a hug before you leave, ok?"

Abby smiled. "I will."

After Trevor's parents left the room, Izzy sat back in her chair and poured herself more wine. "How come he never calls *me* sugar plum?" She held the bottle in the air and motioned toward Abby's glass.

"No. Thanks," Abby replied simply. "I really should get

going." She pushed up from the table. "I have an early flight and a long day ahead of me."

"Oh, come on! I've barely seen you!"

"Sorry Izzy, but I didn't know you were coming, and I've already stayed way longer than I intended. I'll tell you what. Next time I'm in town I'll come down to the city. We'll grab dinner and I'll tell you all about my trip."

"Promise?"

"I promise." Abby laughed. "It was so good to see you! Although, if I'm being honest, I came for the lasagna." She glanced quickly at Trevor, who looked at the table and started to clear his dishes.

Izzy flipped her silky black hair over one shoulder, wagging her perfectly manicured fingernail in Abby and Trevor's direction once again. "I still want to know what the fuck's going on between you two."

"Isa*bel*la!" Renee's voice came ringing out from the kitchen.

"Sorry Mama!" She called back, flipping her palm up and lowering her voice. "You'd never know I was thirty-five years old."

As much as they argued and bantered, this house, this family, had always felt like home to her. There was love here. The kind of deep, authentic love you only got from family.

Izzy was away at school when things went south between her and Trevor. They talked a few times in the first couple of weeks after it happened, but if Izzy knew about the baby, she never said anything. Eventually they lost touch, and Abby couldn't blame her. Blood was thicker than water.

AFTER THE GOODBYES were said and hugs had been both given and received, Abby shrugged into her leather jacket and opened the front door.

"I'll see you, Trev." She looked up at him from under her ball cap and he nodded.

"Safe travels, Abbs. Keep in touch."

Trevor had one arm around Kelsey as they stood on the front porch waving her off. They were going to be just fine without her.

Just fine.

PART II

12

Being on a plane might not be some people's idea of relaxing, but it was the first time in nearly a month that Abby was able to take a deep breath in peace. In Chile she wouldn't have to wonder if Trevor was going to be around the next corner or showing up at her door unannounced. Getting thrown off track wasn't something she could afford at the moment. This next was tour not for beginners. It was both technical and dangerous and would require all her focus.

Although she did her best to screen the group, highly technical rides still put her on edge. She made a point of talking to each person about their experience levels and the types of terrain they were used to. Riders came for the adventure but being in unfamiliar territory, sometimes on unimproved dirt and gravel roads, anything could happen. She'd been lucky so far, but there was a fine line between having a great time on a dual sport and ending up in a cast—or worse. Still, Patagonia was some of the most picturesque riding Abby had ever done, and she couldn't wait to get back on a bike and let the thrum of the engine diffuse the noise inside her head.

On the flight, she was seated between a very large woman

and a very small man. Neither seemed interested in conversation, which was just fine by her. Sleep didn't find her, however, and she got off the plane in Houston frustrated and hungry. She bought an overpriced salad and a glass of wine, trying to relax before the next flight. Last-minute emails from future adventurers kept her busy for a while, but Trevor kept floating in and out of her awareness.

She doodled *Bitches of Steel* on her notepad, then chuckled at herself. She checked her social media accounts and found that Kelsey was doing a fabulous job posting regular photos with engaging captions. There were a lot more likes than normal, probably because Kelsey used at least twice as many hashtags. Engagement was key, and so far, the kid was killing it.

THE FLIGHT TO SANTIAGO, Chile, was happily uneventful. She slept for almost half of the nine-hour flight. It was important to be rested if she was going to ride this route twice in the next two weeks.

Santiago was a beautiful city, full of culture, history, and people like herself from all over the world with a thirst for adventure. The largest and easiest major city to fly into, Santiago was the launching place for all things northern Patagonia. She'd been there once before, so the routine was a bit easier this time.

She always tried to rest for a full day when she arrived in country. It helped combat jet lag and reset her internal clock before getting on a bike and riding in unfamiliar territory. Her routine remained the same no matter where she went, regardless of the time change. Besides, after everything that had happened over the last month, it might take an extra day or two to get in the right headspace.

In Chile's capital, burgeoning with nearly seven million

people, there was no lack of things to see and do. She spent the day wandering the streets taking pictures, and then went to a coffee shop with internet to get some work done. It was easy enough to upload everything to the shared folder Kelsey had created. It remained to be seen whether or not this was a good system, but so far it was working well.

It was surprisingly freeing, knowing someone else was taking care of matching photos to sentiments and posting things to the website. Historically speaking, marketing had been a nightmare due to time constraints and internet availability. Often, by the time she returned from a remote location, the thoughts were out of her head or she had more pressing matters to deal with. She tried outsourcing but had a couple of bad experiences. There were ups and downs to running a business this way, and priorities always dictated.

The rest of the group was meeting her in Pucón, but Abby picked up her BMW 1200GS in Santiago. She had it fitted with a Telepass in order to pay tolls without stopping. Rentals tended to be challenging because she couldn't just pick up a bike in one country and return it in another.

When she first started touring solo, she would purchase a bike outright and then sell it in another country at the end of several months' riding before moving on. Running back-to-back tours didn't afford the time for this kind of luxury.

Multi-week rentals offered better deals than shorter term rentals, but it remained to be seen if this method would be cost effective in the end. This time she planned a three-week rental out of Santiago. Then she would fly to Brazil for another three-week rental, then move on to Costa Rica for the last tour.

She rode from Santiago to Pucón along the Pan-American Highway, which was a ride she hadn't done previously. She stopped frequently, veering off the highway, taking copious notes and pictures along the way, some of which would be good for advertising. The main road was just like any other interstate, but just off the highway were beautiful towns with gorgeous views of the mountains.

She did the ride over two days to allow for stopping and exploration. Lodging was relatively inexpensive and she didn't require much. She often stayed in simple accommodations for a few pesos, always eating locally, as fresh as she could find. Luckily, she had a strong stomach and rarely got sick while traveling.

Pulling off the main highway, she rode west to Concepción on the coast, stopping for pictures at Ramuntcho, a gorgeous, U-shaped cove surrounded by cliffs overlooking a clean white beach. She hiked up onto the rock outcroppings and sat for a while. Mountainous landscapes that ended at the ocean were some of her favorite views, and she took it all in, allowing her body to relax and her mind to let go. Her feet dangled over the edge of the rocks, above the swirling eddies of the Pacific. It was strange sometimes to think this was the same mighty Pacific that crashed the cliffs of Mendocino and traveled in under the Golden Gate Bridge half a world away.

After lunch, she got back on the bike and ventured to los Saltos del Laja, a picturesque waterfall surrounded by horse trails and picnic spots along the Laja River. After capturing a few photos, she rented a cabin nearby. There was a large family gathering happening in the cabin next door, and the smells wafting from their asado were nothing short of mouthwatering. Chilean barbecues were a whole-family affair, a boisterous picnic to be envied by passersby, if for no other reason than the smells coming off the grill.

Meats of all kinds, from pork to rib eye, were grilled up with simple seasonings and served up alongside dishes like Russian salad or ensalada Chileno.

Abby changed into a pair of shorts and a tank top and sat outside on the porch. She enjoyed watching the family next door and hearing the laughter they all shared. *Family*. Family was always a draw, she realized with some sadness.

She was perched on a wooden chair with her feet propped up on the porch railing as children ran circles in the grass and dirt chasing a soccer ball. A man approached her with a plate of food. Chileans tended to be an extremely warm and welcoming. She accepted the plate gratefully.

Chilean Spanish was difficult to understand and nearly impossible for her to speak properly. She wasn't in the habit of turning the *s* sounds into *th* sounds, but she was able to get her thanks across. Through a series of gorilla-like pointing motions that seemed to amuse him, she was able to introduce herself. He kept looking at the motorcycle parked in front of her cabin and wanted to know what she was doing in Chile. She tried to explain using the Spanish she knew without tripping herself up on the dialect and he nodded appropriately, but then he stopped her, holding up his hand, and called out to someone at the barbecue, asking for chicha and some glasses.

"¿Te gustaría un vaso de chicha?" *Would you like a glass of chicha?* A young boy ran over with a bottle fermented, corn-based, alcoholic yumminess and two glasses. He held out a glass and took one for himself.

"Sí, gracias." She smiled gratefully.

Juan sat on the porch step to listen to her story. Relaxed, he ate from his own plate while he listened, smiling and nodding. He seemed to understand her brand of bumbling Spanglish just fine, which was a relief. He let her go on for a good ten minutes before interjecting.

"¿Tienes un pololo?" he asked.

Do I have a what? "¿Pololo? No sé *pololo*," she replied.

"Novio," he clarified, using a more generalized Spanish term instead of what she now realized was undoubtedly Chilean slang.

"A boyfriend? You want to know if I have a boyfriend?" She

laughed out loud, but on the inside the question hung in her mind. No, of course she didn't have a boyfriend. Unless she wanted one, because apparently Trevor was *all in*. "No. No tengo pololo," she answered. "¿Por qué?" *Why?*

"¿Por qué no?" *Why not?*

She laughed again. In her experience, straight Latinos had no problem admitting their attraction, and women were much more likely to be treated as objects here, a fact that Abby had not ever gotten used to. Although she loved so many things about the people and cultures of Latin America, men were considerably more forward—and more tactile—than men back home.

She tried in earnest to study and understand people from different cultures. From food to family and everything in between, it was a continual learning curve. Cultures and social norms were a bit like religion. If you were raised your whole life to believe a certain way, it was easy to see how a worldview could form, but that still didn't make it right. For Abby, the desire to understand and even assimilate cultural norms often butted heads with a desire to fight injustice and change the world.

His question—*why not?*—was valid, but she wasn't sure if he was legitimately paying her a compliment or wondering why he shouldn't ask that question of a woman traveling solo on a motorcycle. She got that question a lot, in fact. Being a fiercely independent woman who spoke her mind was slightly less common in this part of the world. There was a fine line between being rude and making sure that he knew she could hold her own.

When she didn't answer, he held out his hand. "We can start again. I am Juan. It's nice to meet you Abby."

She swallowed her food before shaking hands. "Really? You just let me go on and on and you spoke English the whole time?"

Juan grinned mischievously. "I wanted to see how well you could do in Spanish. It was fine, really."

"I have trouble with the accent here, but this isn't my first time in the country, so I have some practice." She shook her head, embarrassed. "Your English, on the other hand, is very good."

"I own a restaurant just off the highway." He pointed west. "We get a lot of tourists. It helps to speak English. Then more people come to eat there. And you? How did you learn Spanish?"

"I had a friend growing up whose family was from Colombia. Her family spoke mostly Spanish, so I learned a lot just being around them. Then I studied it in school, and it came easily to me. I've done a lot of traveling in Spanish-speaking countries, so I get to practice a lot."

Juan was probably ten years younger than Abby, with a wide mouth and high cheekbones. She could sense the familiar attraction that often came from men who found out she was traveling alone. Apparently, when paired with the motorcycle, this combination was somehow irresistible. Admittedly, it worked in her favor when she was inclined to have some companionship along the road, but today was not one of those days.

After being with Trevor so recently, she couldn't imagine going back to a lifeless, rudimentary orgasm with a stranger. The idea was tempting, but she knew better. That kind of escapism was short-lived, and the need for it hadn't had time to build.

A young, attractive woman walked up and put her arm around his shoulder. "Is my husband bothering you?" she asked.

Abby chuckled as Juan averted his eyes. "No. He was kind enough to offer me some food. Muchísimas gracias," she replied.

The woman also held out her hand by way of introduction. "I am Mia. It's nice to meet you."

"Abby," she replied.

"Is that your motorcycle?" Mia asked, inclining her head toward the BMW.

"For the next three weeks it is, yes."

Mia asked where she was going and when Abby explained about the tour along both sides of the Andes, Mia's eyes showed a thirst for adventure that perhaps Juan was unaware of.

"Do you ride?" Abby asked.

"Me? Oh no." The younger woman dismissed the thought with a wave of her hand. "If something happened to me, who would look after my children?"

It seemed like an old-fashioned idea, but Lauren felt the same way. Abby tried to teach her to ride but she wanted no part of it. Being a mother was important to her, and Abby respected that.

"When I was younger, my brother taught me to ride a smaller type of bike," Mia continued. "We rode in the dirt and through the rocky fields. We were young then."

Abby wondered if Mia considered riding a dream of the past, or if she still secretly wished for the thrill of the throttle. "This bike rides very similarly to the one you probably rode. It just has a lot more power. I'll bet you still know how to ride."

"She doesn't ride." Juan was obviously annoyed by this conversation and said to her in Spanish, "Bring me some more food, would you? I'm still hungry."

"Why don't you come over to el carrete?" Mia asked.

"El carrete?" Abby wasn't familiar with this term. Perhaps it was slang.

"She means the party." Juan got up and walked over to where the children were playing, dismissing her completely. He stole the ball and started playing keep-away, much to the children's delight.

Mia rolled her eyes. "He is like a child. Come, we will have more chicha."

Abby followed Mia over to the party and was introduced to many members of the large gathering. Most of the women spent time serving the men, but then crowding around to listen to Abby. Although Mia was the only one who spoke any English, they all seemed very interested to meet a foreign woman who also spoke Spanish so Abby tried to communicate in their language.

As the hours went by, they kept filling her plate and pouring her glass full of sweetened wine until her belly swelled and her head spun. The party wore into the dark evening hours, and then the music started. There was a fire and dancing and the men broke out the cigars.

Juan offered one to Abby in jest, but she took it anyway, which made Mia laugh hysterically. None of the other women smoked, but Abby pulled her knife out of her pocket and cut the end off her cigar and then asked for a light. All the men stared in disbelief as she puffed it alive and put her feet up on a rock, leaning back in her chair like the rest of them.

"Are you sure you're a woman?" One of the old men smiled through badly decayed teeth.

"Last time I checked," Abby responded, blowing out the smoke like a pro. Mia sat next to her, giggling, but after a few disapproving looks from Juan, she began cleaning up the food.

Abby held her knife up in plain view, inspecting the edges by the light of the fire before stowing the blade and placing it back in her pocket. This was just in case any of the men got any ideas about her locked cabin door in the middle of the night. Thankfully, she'd never been assaulted on a trip, but she'd learned rather quickly that sending a clear message was an effective deterrent—especially when alcohol was involved, which tended to make poor decision-makers out of otherwise decent men.

Juan's question about her boyfriend status came back around from an old man sitting to her right. "You're so beautiful. Do you have a man that you travel with?" he asked her in Spanish.

"I prefer to travel with women," she answered, which elicited a lot of snickering from the other men, who probably wondered if she was a lesbian. Let them think what they wanted. She wasn't about to get into a discussion about gender or sexuality. There was nothing wrong with being a lesbian, after all. She relaxed while the men told stories. They talked very fast, and between the lack of *s* sounds and the alcohol, she could only understand bits and pieces.

All in all, it was a lovely evening. She had intended to make an instant meal in her Jetboil. Instead she was treated to a veritable feast, complete with a good quality cigar. It was just this sort of chance encounter that made travel and exploration her favorite pastime. She learned more about a country and its people by watching and listening around the fire than she ever could by reading a travel guide.

EARLY THE NEXT MORNING, she was just finishing her coffee and packing out the bike when Mia came over with some food in warm towels. She unwrapped it to reveal two slices of homemade bread spread with dulce de leche, an addictive substance resembling caramel but less sweet and far tastier. She apologized that the bread was yesterday's because she couldn't bake when the family was camping.

"This is so kind of you, really! I'll have them at my first stop!" Abby put the slices together into a sandwich and carefully tucked them into the insulated food compartment in her tank bag.

"I want you to know I admire what you are doing, giving women a chance to see our beautiful country." Mia had written the name and address of their restaurant on some paper and invited Abby to come any time with the women from her tours. "We have some rooms we rent above the restaurant. If you want to stay, let me know."

Abby took the paper gratefully. "Thank you! I will. Do you have an email address?"

Mia smiled and nodded, pulling a pen out of her apron pocket and adding her restaurant email to the piece of paper.

"I'll be in touch."

Mia looked over her shoulder at the bike all loaded out and ready to travel. Her eyes grew wide. "Have an adventure for me too!"

Abby had watched Mia with her children the evening before. She laughed with them and disciplined them and hugged them and tickled them until they wiggled out of her grasp. She was a good mother, and her children obviously adored her. She didn't act as if she regretted her choices, it was just that, faced with a big adventure, we all tend to wish ourselves a part of it.

Mia didn't want to give up being a mom to her children to travel the world on a motorcycle. But for her, and a lot of women like her, the thought of stepping away from their everyday lives for a week or two and going on a grand adventure was a thrilling prospect. Even Lauren had said as much the night before she left.

The reviews people left on her website said their time with Steel Journeys helped them to remember who they were on the inside. The part of them that existed before they gave their lives to their jobs or their families. It reminded them not to lose sight of their dreams, and that freedom didn't have to mean abandoning their lives completely.

Granted, her tours were expensive, and not something that Mia's family would likely be able to support. She met women all the time who would love to travel but didn't have the means. She had even considered trying to get donations for a scholarship fund to help women who couldn't otherwise participate for financial reasons, but she just wasn't there yet. There were so many things she wanted to do with her company, but right now it was just one step at a time.

Abby tried to give back where she could by supporting organizations that gave women a hand up and taught them business skills. In fact, she was planning to visit one in Jaco when she got to Costa Rica.

Abby gave Mia a hug and climbed onto the bike. She buckled into her helmet and started the engine, wishing she could make it quieter for those who were still sleeping. As she started to pull away, two of the children ran out of the cabin next door in their pajamas. They all waved goodbye, and soon Abby was back on the road.

She was so thankful to have met Mia and Juan and their families. That was how most of her connections ended up being made, and why she was able to give the women on her tours a deeply human experience. Almost everywhere Abby went she tried to make honest and authentic connections, and this was evident to the women who traveled with her. Somehow, it opened them up to a level of connection they had lost along the way, not only with others, but with themselves as well.

A picture was framed in her mind of Mia with an arm around each of her children. It wasn't so strange, she realized, the way Trevor made memories in his head. It was how the mind and heart held onto the things that touched them deeply.

She continued south for a couple of hours, enjoying the

quiet of the early morning. Although the Pan-American was a busy, multi-lane highway, traffic was a non-issue on a weekday in the late spring before the tourist season really ramped up.

She stopped at Cerro Ñielol in Temuco and hiked up to an overlook with sweeping panoramic views. Here she enjoyed the dulce de leche and bread from Mia and a few handfuls of nuts from her bag. She took some pictures and with a surprisingly strong cell signal decided to take the opportunity to upload some photos to the cloud for Kelsey to retrieve.

It was such a strange concept, things hanging out in the cloud. She imagined a satellite up in space, storing data and then beaming it back down wherever in the world it was needed. She had her laptop open when a notification sounded in her messenger app.

It was Trevor.

Kelsey said you just added some photos. I'm hoping you don't mind if I edit a few of them.

Is Kelsey giving you a cut of her monthly stipend? Abby fired back.

No, but that's not a bad idea. Maybe I'll ask her, he replied.

I appreciate your offer, but I'm sure you have better things to do with your time.

Are you?

She sat munching on cashews and thinking about his question. In reality, she didn't have any idea what he did with his time. She typed: *Well then, I guess what you do with your time is your business, even if that ends up helping me with mine.*

It was a convoluted way of saying it, but he must have gotten the message because he typed back: *I like to think of it more as me helping Kelsey. If she's successful at helping you, she keeps her job, which keeps her happy, which makes me happy.*

There was a brief pause and then he typed: *Win. Win... Win* and added a trophy emoji.

She closed her laptop, trying to shut him out, which was

getting admittedly more difficult as time went on. She wanted to help Kelsey, but she needed him out of her head. Being friends was fine conceptually but putting theory into practice was proving difficult.

All those years he was out of sight and out of mind, a lesson in bad decision making that formed the core of how she saw the world. He was a whisper of a memory. An apparition. But when Trevor's ghost took on flesh and blood, the real haunting began. Now she couldn't shake him, even half a world away.

Once the tour began, she would be too busy to think about any of it, but for the next ten days she was all by herself, with nothing but mountains and miles of road, and twenty-five hours in the saddle. Luckily, riding was the one thing that helped her to forget whatever it was that was nagging at her thoughts. The nights would be long, but at least the days would be easy.

The road soothed her nerves, no matter how frazzled they became. It calmed her soul and silenced the voices, like a drug that she needed more than she was willing to admit. She took a deep breath, packed everything up, and hopped back in the saddle. *One day at a time, Abby. One day at a time.*

13

Abby arrived in Pucón in the late afternoon. It was a picturesque mountain town nestled at the foot of an active volcano called Villarrica on the shores of a lake by the same name. Nicknamed the Adventure Capital of Chile, Pucón attracted outdoor enthusiasts of all kinds, from kayakers to mountain climbers and everything in between. Situated in the beautiful Chilean Lakes District, Pucón was bursting with tourists from all over the world. She checked in at the hotel where her group would be staying and took some time to talk to the manager about their schedule.

She spent the next week riding the route they would take from Pucón. South along Route 5 until it became the Carretera Austral, or the southern highway, which then followed Route 7 through some of the most breathtaking and varied terrain on the planet. From pristine mountain lakes to volcanos, this tour had everything a rider could want, at times following the ocean, and at others winding deep into the mountains.

There were plenty of challenging dirt and gravel roads for these adventure babes, who would be exclusively riding dual sports for this trip. She chose a BMW, but most of her riders would be on smaller Honda CB500Xs or Africa Twins. They were lightweight, agile, and easy to pick up when dropped.

Abby made a habit of staying at all the designated places beforehand, making sure that the hosts were prepared for their arrival and giving them a little extra business to boot. She finalized room rates and discussed all the details down to food allergies, which were a frequent challenge. She wanted the women to feel welcomed and cared for, even if that meant an endless list of logistics to wade through.

She even went to local businesses and arranged for perks like specials on food and activities, and helped advertise the local shops, then arranged for vouchers and fliers to be placed in baskets in each room upon their arrival. Tourism was the best income many of these towns had, and she liked to encourage support of the local economy.

She always followed up with each business afterward with a personal note thanking them and asking them to remember her in the future. It was a small gesture, but a personal one, and it made all the difference.

This time, she was asking the businesses if she could leave a small decal with the Steel Journeys logo and website in the window of each shop so that her group could find the places easier by looking for the decal. Whether or not they kept the decals up after the tour remained to be seen, but for those businesses that did, it was free advertising for her. Win. Win... Win.

There were multiple ferry crossings, and as she went, she gave the ferry companies the information about their dates and verified the reservations for all ten bikes in advance to make sure they would get on all together.

Aside from some inevitable construction delays, plus rain and lower temperatures through the mountain passes on the way into Argentina, the pre-ride portion through Chile went smoothly. This was why she chose the BMW. Heated grips made all the difference, since her hands tended to get cold and stay cold. She also made a point of bringing gear that was compatible with the bike—a GPS, adapters, and some options for USB and solar charging.

It wasn't exactly an off-the-grid system, but then again, running a global business meant needing to be available to customers, especially when running back-to-back tours. She still used the locator on a daily basis for Lauren, and apparently Kelsey was tracking her now too, creating a "real time" tour map that visitors to the website could click on to "Follow Abby and Her Crew."

The Argentinian side was a whole other world of riding. The winds were a formidable enemy and downright dangerous at times, but it was worth staring down the enemy, because Route 40 was one of the most beautiful stretches of riding in the world.

By the time she arrived in the picturesque, Swiss-style town of San Carlos de Bariloche, her nerves were fried from white-knuckling the bike. For the first time ever, she considered a midstream route reversal. Winds buffeted her predominantly from the north and west, which would mean a headwind on the way back up. It was a tough decision, because the last time she was on this route, the weather cooperated just fine. Maybe talking to locals would help.

Windy mountain passes were one thing but endangering her clients was another. According to the questionnaires she sent out, this particular group was well seasoned, and all had experience off-road, but it was impossible to predict the weather conditions, especially in the mountains.

At an elevation just shy of three thousand feet, San Carlos de Bariloche was like a postcard, perched in the middle of the Lakes District and overlooking Nahuel Huapi National Park. She turned down Calle Bmé Mitre, the main street of the town, and looked for a place to park, but the road was packed with people and cars. A stranger started waving her arms, indicating an impossibly small space that would never fit a car, but she was able to maneuver the bike in just fine.

Abby cut the engine and took off her helmet. The woman was still standing on the sidewalk. "Gracias, señora."

"De nada." The woman smiled. "I like your bike. I used to have one just like it."

"Oh, you speak English!" Abby smiled.

"Yes." She laughed. "It's an occupational hazard. I travel for work. Where are you from?"

"California."

"You're a long way from home."

"Yes. Yes, I am."

"My name is Elena." She stuck out her hand and Abby shook it.

"Abby Steel."

"That sounds like a movie star name."

"I assure you, I am nobody famous. Just Abby."

"What brings you to Bariloche?"

"I'm just passing through right now. But I'll be coming back again in a week or so leading a group of women on a motorcycle tour through northern Patagonia."

"No kidding! That sounds like so much fun!"

"It is." Abby smiled. "I keep going to sleep thinking I have the best job on the planet, and when I wake up the dream is still real."

"I'll bet!" Elena laughed. "Where are you headed now?"

"I just need to find some dinner. Can you recommend a good place? Preferably someplace not too touristy?"

"I can, yes. I was just about to get some dinner myself. What do you say I take you to the same place I am going? Perhaps we can share a table?"

"Sure. Is it far?"

"It's just down this road here. Come, I'll show you."

"Perfect, thanks." Abby stowed her gear and the two women started walking.

Elena was a few years older than Abby, maybe mid-forties, with a kind smile and bouncy brown curls that jiggled when she walked. Despite her diminutive height she carried a large presence.

They turned down one of the side streets and soon they were standing in front of a drab stone building that didn't look like much from the outside. Elena pushed open the large, heavy wooden door with iron handles and their senses were immediately assaulted with rich, tantalizing smells.

"I hope you like meat!" Elena laughed. "We Argentinians love our beef."

Abby knew this about the Argentinian culture, and tried her best to be respectful, but between the unbelievable wines and the sizable portions of red meat, her body sometimes complained or downright revolted. Years of travel had taught her a lot about her body. She didn't do well on a continuous diet of rich foods, heavy meats, and alcohol—not to mention her rule about drinking and riding.

The tables were elegantly set with white linens and sparkling crystal, and every square inch of the place from floor to ceiling was hung with lush greenery and plants, making the entire space feel as if it were outdoors instead of in. It buzzed with life and energy, as if they'd closed the door on the serene, lakeside town and entered a place that was altogether different.

Elena seemed to know the people who worked at this restaurant and was able to secure a premium table upstairs with a view. She got hugs from almost every server as they walked through the crowded establishment, weaving their way past crowded tables with lively patrons.

Just twenty minutes away was Cerro Catedral, which boasted some of the best skiing in all of South America, and all the other businesses in this mountain town vied for tourists with the après-ski culture. This little restaurant was jam packed and yet there were very few tourists, a welcome relief for Abby, who preferred smaller venues with local flavor.

"So tell me, how is it that you know everyone here?" Abby asked as they were seated.

"This restaurant is owned by my cousin. She is a wonderful woman and I wish you could meet her, but she is not here today." Elena answered. "I used to work here, over the winters, during ski season."

"That makes sense." Abby smiled. "And what is it you do now for work?"

"I work for my other cousin," Elena answered. "She designs and sells ski apparel for women."

"Only for women?"

Elena nodded.

"Are all the women in your family powerful and business-savvy?

"No, but they are the ones I choose to spend my time with." Elena smiled. The waiter came by to pour water and set a bottle of wine between them, even though they hadn't asked for any.

Abby inclined her head toward the bottle. "One of the perks of knowing the owner?"

"I'm afraid so. Would you like some?" Elena started to pick up the bottle but Abby put her hand over her glass.

"I wish I could, but I still need to ride after this and find my hotel. I never drink until I've finished riding for the day."

"I wish more Argentinians would feel the same as you. Too many accidents happen. I respect your decision."

"Don't let me stop you, though. It looks wonderful. Please —partake."

Elena shook her head. "I wouldn't want to be rude—we'll send it back. There's more to a good dinner than wine. Now, if you tell me you don't eat meat, we might have a hard time at this restaurant!" She laughed.

"To be honest, when I'm home I don't eat a lot of meat, but when I travel, I always try the local dishes. It's hard to recommend a good meal to my clients if I've never eaten the food myself."

"I'm relieved to hear that." Her eyes twinkled. "I don't know how I would've explained to my cousin that we came to her restaurant and didn't drink wine *or* eat meat."

Abby smiled as she perused the menu, thankful to see a few seafood dishes. "Don't get too excited just yet... This trout looks divine."

Elena peeked over the top of Abby's menu, to see what she was looking at. "Oh, you're right. That is actually quite good. The sauce that the chef uses is to die for."

"Sounds perfect."

"How long have you been doing this?" Elena put her elbows up on the table and folded her hands underneath her chin.

"Riding? Or leading tours?"

"Both. Either. Pick one." Elena turned her palms up.

"I've been riding since I was a teenager. Leading tours for the last couple of years."

"And what made you want to do this as a job?"

"My father once told me that if you could find something you love to do and then get someone to pay you to do it, you would never hate your job."

"Did your father hate his job?"

"I think my father hated a lot of things, but he loved fixing cars. It was just hard on his body. Anyway, after he died, I spent a lot of time traveling by myself, thinking about what I wanted out of life."

"How long ago was that?"

"Three years ago."

"I'm so sorry."

"Thank you. I miss them both very much."

"Both?"

"My parents both died together in a car accident."

Elena's hand covered her mouth. "Oh goodness. That must have been terrible."

"I started riding solo, all over the world. Then I decided to start this company to share with other women all the amazing things I've seen and experienced."

"You have your own company?" Elena's eyebrows went up. "That's wonderful." She raised her water glass in a toast. "To powerful women."

"To powerful women."

Most of the time, Abby didn't feel particularly powerful. She was just doing what was in her heart, but other people always made a big deal about it. Truth be told, she was a bit of a control freak and she knew it. It was easier to run her own company than to work for someone else. After they finished ordering their food, Abby's phone vibrated, and a photo appeared on the screen. It was Kelsey and Trevor, arm-in-arm in front of a drivers ed training school. Abby and Elena both glanced at the phone at the same time.

"Is that your daughter and husband?"

Abby quickly shook her head. "No! No, it's just a friend."

"You are not married?"

"No, I'm not."

"May I see the picture again?" Elena asked.

Abby retrieved the photo and turned the screen toward Elena, who picked up the phone and studied it. "Whoever she is, she looks very happy in this picture. Why did she send it?"

"The short answer? I promised I would teach her how to ride a motorcycle after she took the required courses."

"And the long answer?" Elena asked, a smile tugging at her lips.

"Would require this bottle of wine and maybe another." Abby laughed.

"I thought so." Elena set the phone down. "He's very handsome."

"Yes. He is that." Abby sipped her water and tried to change the subject. "You said you have a bike like the one I'm riding?"

"Had. A long time ago."

"Tell me about it—How long have you been riding?"

"Hmm. Let me see. I guess since I was...about the age of your friend's daughter. I grew up riding through these mountains with my brothers and cousins."

"Not your sisters?"

"I don't have any sisters. Just cousins. And good friends."

"I'm so jealous. I love these mountains. I could sit all day and just look at them. Is it still beautiful to you? Or does it fade into the background?"

"Rain or shine, wind or snow, it is beautiful, always. I try not to take it for granted."

"The wind has just been killing me today!"

"Oh." Elena threw up her hands in disgust. "It's terrible, isn't it? I never get used to it. Even though I know it's coming, it seems to come from nowhere and then, like a ghost, it disappears."

"I'm a little perplexed, because the last time I rode this loop, I don't remember the winds being so fierce. It's doable, but I don't want to put people in danger."

"I'm not sure when you were riding here last, but the gods must've been smiling on you. This side of the Andes is well known for terrible winds."

"I do remember that from my research, but then like I said, when I rode it, the wind was not a big issue. I never gave it another thought and went ahead and planned the tour to start in Pucón, but to travel south on the Chilean side first and then come north up the Argentinian side."

"It does depend somewhat on the time of year. Spring is the worst, but it would probably be better to drive south on this side first. Then again, no one can predict the weather and some days it is good, and some days it is not so good. When you ride a bike, you take your chances, no?"

Elena was right, but it wasn't like Abby to make mistakes in her planning. She always did a considerable amount of research and considered all the factors, especially weather. Now she had to decide: should she try to reverse-engineer the trip and change all her reservations, or was it too late?

"You are continuing north from here? Going back to Pucón?" Elena asked.

"That's the plan."

"Why don't you finish the trip before you decide? You still have many miles ahead of you, and the weather can be different in different regions."

Elena was right. Abby decided to try to put it out of her head. They talked about riding and clothing design and even politics. Soon they were eating dessert and almost two hours had gone by.

"What a wonderful meal. You were right about the fish—it was incredible. I'm putting this restaurant on my tour list."

"I have so enjoyed talking to you, Abby. It feels impossible that we've just met. You're very easy to talk to."

"Thank you. You as well." Abby leaned back in her chair. "I'm so glad you found me that parking spot."

"I think I'd like to come on one of your tours some time." she replied. "Do you have a business card?"

"Yes, of course." Abby reached into her jacket and pulled out a card. "Where would you like to go?"

"Somewhere that is *not* in South America. Like maybe Egypt."

"Hmm." Abby nodded. "I haven't been there yet."

"Really?" Elena smiled.

"I'll do some research. Safety might be an issue, depending on the political climate, but I'll look into it! I'll be sure to let you know what I decide. What's your second choice?"

"I've never been to Spain. I hear wonderful things about Madrid."

"I can definitely make that happen—next year, in fact. Check the website." Abby handed her a card.

"I have a friend who I think would want to come along, but we will both need to brush up on our riding skills."

"The more, the merrier!" Abby started, but then she corrected herself. "Actually, that's not true. I generally cap tours at ten people."

"Then I will be the first to sign up to make sure I get a spot."

"Deal."

"Now..." Elena once again put her elbows on the table and leaned forward. "Tell me about the handsome man in the picture. What is his name?"

"Wouldn't you rather talk about motorcycles?"

Elena laughed, shaking her head.

"His name is Trevor," Abby stated, trying to keep her emotions from coloring her tone.

"And how did you two meet?"

"How did we meet?" Abby blew the air out of her cheeks. "Well, we dated for about three years when we were much younger. Then, I didn't see him for many years. He came back into my life unexpectedly a few weeks ago." Telling a stranger about Trevor seemed safer somehow. Like talking to a bartender or your hairdresser.

"And he is single? Where is the girl's mother?"

"She died recently."

"Oh my. That's terrible. And your feelings for this Trevor are still strong, are they not?"

"Yes. They are." Abby hated admitting it, but it was the truth.

"And does he share your feelings?"

"He does." Abby sipped her water.

"So, what is the problem?"

When she explained it out loud it didn't seem out of the ordinary. Old acquaintances often met up again later in life and formed romantic relationships. What exactly *was* the problem?

"He had sex with my best friend. That's what ended the relationship. His daughter is the result of that betrayal."

Elena nodded sympathetically. "I see. That does make it complicated. But that was a long time ago, no?"

"Yes."

"Some hurts take longer than others to get over," Elena replied, putting her hand over Abby's and patting it like a mother would. "I will have to ask you again when we get to Egypt or Spain or wherever it is I decide to go riding with you."

"I'm not sure I'll have anything new to tell you, but feel free to ask."

It sounded so petty, letting the past dictate the future. She felt foolish, hanging onto her justifications like that. Thankfully, Elena changed the subject.

"Where are you staying?"

When Abby told her, she gave Abby very specific directions about how to get there and where to park her bike safely.

"I really should be getting over there before it gets too dark to find my way."

"I understand." Elena gave her a business card and made Abby promise to email her when the Egypt tour dates were settled.

Abby asked if she thought Elena's cousin would be willing to put one of her decals in the window of the restaurant if she promised to recommend it to her group.

"Of course she would!" Elena smiled. "In fact, I will put it there myself."

Abby pulled a decal from the inner pocket of her jacket and handed it across the table. The two women walked downstairs together. Elena whispered something to the restaurant manager, who nodded.

"Don't we have to pay?" Abby wondered.

"The meal is on me," Elena answered. "And I won't let you argue about it."

"Thank you—for everything. You've been so kind."

"It is my pleasure. I'm so glad to have met you." Elena stuck the decal in the window and smiled. "There! It's done."

"Thanks again. This place was a real find." They exchanged hugs and soon Abby was back on her way, feeling once again like she had made a new friend in a foreign country.

The hotel was easy to find with Elena's directions, and when she arrived, she was presented with a bottle of wine.

"This is for you ma'am. Compliments of your new friend." The kindness of strangers never ceased to amaze her, and she opened the wine on the balcony, looking out over the bustling town. That night she slept with the doors open, and in the morning the cold mountain air woke her, along with a text from Trevor and another photo from their ride to Mendocino.

Thinking of you as you adventure on and remembering with fondness our special day together. Safe travels, Abby.

She lay in bed for a long time, looking at the photo, and allowed herself just a few minutes to relive the time they spent together. It was so easy, being with him. Why was it also the hardest thing she had ever done?

14

Just as Elena predicted, the rest of the route was different, and the weather changed dramatically from one section of road to the next. The rest of the pre-ride went smoothly, and when she got back to Pucón, she had a couple of days to rest before everyone arrived in Temuco, about an hour and a half north.

After Bariloche, she took a lot of notes and a lot of photos, but the Wi-Fi had been sketchy, so she spent the entire afternoon in a sidewalk café drinking coffee and using their internet to upload dozens of photos. These would be added to each location on an interactive real-time map so that when the tour was happening, potential riders could see what it looked like at each stop on the journey.

Kelsey set up one of the spreadsheets they'd discussed. It was well organized and formatted exactly for her needs. She had to hand it to Kelsey. The girl had fantastic ideas, although at times her emails also seemed to have a heavy Trevor influence. Either he was feeding her ideas, or the apple didn't fall far from the tree. Either way, she received regular communications a couple of times a week, just like they'd agreed.

Kelsey was holding up her end of the bargain, and in fact, the website had never looked so good. The logo Kelsey designed was now part of a banner on the home page, and she added a few of the best testimonials right on the front page in a rotating gallery of photos with the quotes beside them. That way, visitors saw pictures of real riders and read what they thought of the tours as soon as they clicked on the front page. The number of comments, as well as the number of inquiries, was picking up, so it seemed to be working.

The next day was a true day off, so Abby decided to do something completely different, and take an excursion trip up to one of the thermal spas in the mountains of Villarrica National Park. The hotel offered transportation, so she grabbed her small bag with a bathing suit, flip-flops, and her travel towel and ventured up into the hills.

"Have you ever been to this spa before?" A man across the aisle of the shuttle asked. He spoke English to her, which many people did if they could.

"No," she answered.

He looked a lot like Juan from los Saltos del Laja when he smiled. Straight white teeth, wavy brown hair, dark eyes, and high cheekbones. He was traveling alone, and she noticed neither a ring nor a tan line from where he had taken one off to meet women.

"You're in for a treat." He smiled. "This is the most beautiful spa in the area."

"I heard that as well. Have you been before?"

"Oh, yes." He nodded. "I come here for work almost every month and I always visit this spa."

The other people in the van began asking the man questions about his experience and she listened half-heartedly. Her mind was elsewhere as she stared out the window. The road was steep, and as it wound its way deeper into the mountains she got lost in the landscape and tried to let go of everything except the moment. The road turned rough about halfway up, and the thought crossed her mind as she bounced in her seat that she might have been better off taking the bike. Its shocks were made for roads like this and the van's were not.

Her mind began to wander as they rolled on through the thickly wooded roads that made up Villarrica National Park. Perhaps this would be one more experience she could personally recommend to other riders on the days that bridged the tour. It was hard not to always be thinking about the business. Even when she was *off*, she was always looking for new adventures to recommend to women who wanted to experience something completely outside their normal life.

Going to the top of a mountain to soak in a hot spring that was carved into the lush, forested landscape had to top that list. Or maybe that was Abby projecting her own love of hot soaks and a longing for home. She wanted to escape real life for a while too, and nothing sounded better at the moment than to sink into the warm, hidden pools and soothe her aching muscles.

Ten days of hard riding was therapy for her mind, but her body still felt the effects. Hiking, riding, and camping kept her body active and her joints mobile, but it was an achier end to the journeys these days. She wondered, for the first time since she'd started the business, what the end of this road might look like.

Someday, riding a dual sport through gravel and dirt on poorly maintained mountain roads might not hold the charm it did today. Still, there would be plenty of time for paved roads in the future. All the more reason to travel these roads now, while she was still young enough to endure the challenges.

"What brings you to Chile?" the man with the warm smile was asking. The chatter had died down in the rest of the van.

"I'm leading a motorcycle tour through northern Patagonia."

She expected the usual surprised gasp or disbelieving laughter. Instead the man smiled. "That's excellent. What do you ride?"

"For this tour? A BMW 1200GS," she said, grabbing onto the seat in front of her as she bounced into the air again. "Which I daresay would have been a more comfortable ride than this."

"And when you're at home, wherever that is, what do you ride then?"

"Currently, a Harley Davidson, but I've ridden a lot of different bikes over the years. And home is a little bit of everywhere these days."

The man nodded and laughed in agreement, then he stuck his hand across the aisle. "I'm Juan."

"You too?" she blurted.

"¿Perdón?"

"Nothing. I just—seem to meet a lot of men named Juan in my travels in this part of the world."

"Ah, yes. It is a very popular name."

"I'm Abby."

"It's enchanting to meet you, Abby."

She had always loved the way some words, when translated from Spanish to English, felt classy and genteel. Enchanting was one of those words.

Just then, another woman tapped him on the shoulder and asked a few more questions, which thankfully took him a long time to answer. By the time they'd finished their conversation, the van was pulling into the entrance to the hot springs. Talk about enchanting! Red boardwalks wound their way through slate pools carved into the natural landscape.

According to the brochure, there were twenty different pools to choose from. Although it was a bit hectic getting checked in, once she was wandering the grounds in a cozy robe that covered her bathing suit, the questions filling her mind over the last several weeks began to fall away.

Dipping her toes into a soothing pool with a waterfall crashing down the mountain right next to her, time slowed. If she couldn't be on a bike, water was the next best go-to when things got rough or she needed to think. The ocean, a river, or her own bathtub—warm water washed everything away. Lowering the rest of her body into the warm spring, she let herself relax, and for the next hour or more she didn't think about Trevor or Kelsey or her parents or Lauren or anyone coming to town the following day. She simply thought about how good the water felt and how grateful she was to be alive.

The hot springs were truly a magical experience. She soaked, ate lunch, and then soaked some more. When she finally relaxed to the point where her muscles felt like tubs of Jell-O, she started cataloguing details about the venue, exploring the boardwalks, taking lots of pictures, and asking questions about package options and which were the busiest days and months of the year. While it seemed counterintuitive to do work while trying to have a relaxing day off, this gem was too good not to share. It was recommendations of hidden gems like these springs that meant great reviews and word of mouth referrals.

On the way back, the seating arrangements changed, and Juan sat next to her. He had left her alone all day at the thermal pools and for that she was grateful. Perhaps he wasn't trying to pick her up after all. The mountain road was dark and the driver seemed more inclined to avoid the larger potholes this time. Abby began to doze in the seat, but every time she got close to going out, a big rut would jolt her awake.

She decided to strike up a conversation with Juan, who was sitting quietly next to her, minding his own business.

"So what is it you do for work that brings you to Pucón so often?"

"I lead motorcycle tours."

"You do not!" She laughed.

"No, really! I do. We ride north and cut across the Andes into Argentina, then ride south along Route 40 and then cross back over and come up this side."

"Well, my group is going south down the Chilean side first. Maybe we can wave to one another as we pass."

He laughed. "Perhaps we will. Now tell me, and please do not be offended, but I don't see many women riders out there. Are you the only woman who rides in your groups?"

"No." She shook her head. "The group is all women."

Juan looked surprised by this. "You are not allowed to take men with you? What kind of a boss makes rules like that?"

She ignored the boss comment. "I prefer all-female groups."

"You are a lesbian?" he asked.

"No." She gave him half a smirk.

"I'm afraid I don't understand." Juan's face contorted as the truth dawned on him. "You're the boss, aren't you?"

"Bingo!"

"And you ride with women on purpose." He shook his head, embarrassed. "I'm sorry. I feel I have given offense."

"Don't worry about it. I get that all the time."

A short but awkward silence ensued as Juan tried to keep the conversation going. "I do a tour every month on this route when the weather is good like this. Some are shorter, some longer. How long have you been leading tours in Chile?"

"This is my second time riding this particular route, but I lead tours all over the world."

"Really? That's fascinating. Tell me about the places you've gone. I have nothing but time and a bouncy road to keep my mind occupied." He gestured around the darkened van.

She listed the global destinations she had ridden over the past several years, and then lumped all her US travel in at the end.

"So you have crossed the United States on your motorcycle as well?"

"Twice across and once diagonally." She nodded.

"Where has a woman like you been all of my life?" He laughed.

"At the risk of offending you right back, I'm surprised that a strong, independent woman is something you find desirable."

"My mother was an independent woman, God rest her soul." He crossed himself and kissed his fingers.

"You said you come here once a month for work. Where do you come here from?"

"I live in Spain half of the year."

"I love Spain. What part are you from?"

"Madrid."

"Such a vibrant city. And Reina Sofía is hands-down my favorite museum. In fact, I never knew I liked modern art until I walked into that building. I didn't want to leave!"

"A woman with impeccable taste who also rides a motorcycle." He shook his head. "I say again to you, where have you been all my life?" It was more of an expression than a pickup line, accompanied by his warm, friendly laugh.

His demeanor was relaxed and friendly, and it put Abby at ease, which didn't happen very often while she was traveling. He seemed content to have a simple conversation and she was enjoying talking to someone with shared interests. Of course, they were trapped on a shuttle bus in the gathering darkness.

"What brought you here to Chile?" she asked.

"In Madrid there are a surprising number of Argentinians. I met so many people who spoke so highly of their country that I had to come and visit. Now I spend my winters here, between Argentina and Chile, because here—it is summer."

"And then you return to Spain?"

"Yes."

"Do you lead tours there as well?"

"No, but I should. I've been everywhere on my motorcycle."

"I think I have a group starting out of Madrid in May next year."

"I would love to give you some suggestions on where to go. There are many hidden gems that I'm certain are not part of the normal tour routes."

"That would be fantastic! Thank you."

"We will have to exchange information."

"Ok."

Leads like this made all the difference. Personal touches, authentic relationships, and best-kept secrets helped make her tours memorable, and it all started with connections like this.

A few minutes later the shuttle pulled up to the hotel in Pucón. There Juan kept his promise and merely requested to exchange information. He didn't come on to her or ask her for a drink, although he seemed like he wanted to. Oddly enough, the simple fact that he *didn't* come on to her was a little bit of a turn on.

There were worse things than spending a pleasant evening in the company of an articulate and personable man, so she took a shot. "I'm going to have a drink at the bar. Would you like to join me?"

"I'd be delighted." He nodded appreciatively.

The bar had high-backed stools. He pulled hers out for her. "Thank you." She smiled. "Although, that wasn't necessary."

"Perhaps I'm old fashioned, but I was taught to treat a woman like a lady. Please. Allow me this indulgence."

"Fair enough."

They ordered a bottle of Tempranillo and sat at the bar, talking and laughing about different places they'd been and things they'd seen. They exchanged solo travel horror stories of swamp crossings and venomous snakes and torrential downpours that came out of nowhere. The only place she had him was the grizzly sighting. Not many of those where he'd been riding.

"Tell me how close you were to the grizzly bear." He drained his wine.

"I don't know. Maybe two hundred yards? Um, meters. Close enough to be thankful I was on a straight road with a powerful engine."

"Were you afraid?"

"Hell yeah, I was afraid. Wouldn't you be?"

"Terrified, yes." He laughed, pouring out the rest of the bottle.

Abby excused herself to use the restroom and when she came back, she spied the empty bottle. "We should get more," she announced.

"What time do your ladies arrive?" He asked.

"In the afternoon," she replied. "Why, are you going to send me to bed?"

He took her hand. "If I can be honest, I would like nothing more than to *take* you to bed. I am, as I said before, enchanted by you, Abby Steel." He said her name slowly so that he could pronounce it correctly. "But I also respect that you have a business to run and a job to do, and so do I. And those things will not be easy with a hangover."

"That has got to be the nicest refusal I have ever received." Honestly, his passive flirting and genuine restraint was still turning her on, and the wine wasn't helping matters.

"I am not refusing you." He brought her hand to his lips. "I am merely stating the obvious. More wine is not necessary and may in fact impair our ability to truly enjoy the rest of the evening." He released her hand and didn't try to touch her again. He merely picked up his wine and smiled into the glass.

A man who didn't want to drink more because it would make the sex less enjoyable? He *was* talking about sex, wasn't

LYNDA MEYERS

he? Abby's head was fuzzy. He was absolutely right, she realized. More wine would make things worse.

"The rest of the evening?" Her eyes narrowed.

His head tilted slightly as he attempted to gauge her reaction. "I am perfectly free until the day after tomorrow, so what happens tonight is entirely up to you. I have no expectations. I am simply grateful to have met you and to have spent time with such an alluring and exquisite woman."

Was this guy even for real? "So I could say goodnight right now, put my money on the bar, and walk away...and you would be happy?"

"No. I would not be happy," Juan replied. "First of all, I would never allow you to pay for the wine."

"And second?"

"I've never met a woman quite like you. I want to keep looking at you. Talking to you. You are a strong, intelligent, bewitching woman. But that's not all I see."

This was no pickup. He was utterly wooing her. "What else do you see, Juan?" she asked.

"I see a woman who spends a lot of time alone. Who has no *need* for a man, but a desire all the same. And I see the war that wages in her soul."

For some reason his words pricked her heart, and hot tears stung her eyes without her permission. "I think I need to go to bed now."

Juan stood. Pulling a large wad of money out of his pocket, he counted out a few bills to leave on the bar. "Please. Allow me to escort you to your room."

"I'm a big girl. I know the way."

"I promise I will leave you quietly at your door without argument."

She didn't answer him directly, but neither did she refuse. She simply started walking and he fell into step, one hand at her elbow and the other in the small of her back. She was still

198

close to tears and couldn't understand why. Suddenly she didn't want to spend the night alone. If that meant being in the arms of a stranger, then so be it, but she sure as hell didn't want to be a pity case either.

Abby, what the fuck is wrong with you?

15

When they got to the door of her room, she put the key in the lock but didn't turn the handle. When she turned to face him, his hands were folded behind his back as if he were part of the royal guard and was seeing a princess to her chambers.

"Abby, it was such a delight meeting you." He nodded politely.

Her eyes were still rimmed with tears.

"What is it? What is wrong?" He stepped closer and reached both hands up to cup her face, with no regard to the physical boundary that, seconds before, he'd been intent on maintaining. Her tears had changed the game. He was gentle. Kind.

She shook her head within his hands and one tear slipped out of her eye. He pulled her head into his chest and held her for a moment. "Would you like me to come in?"

She just nodded and he reached behind her, twisting the handle and spinning her softly in the direction of the open door. He asked permission to use her bathroom and when he came out, he found her sitting on the edge of the bed, staring out at the city lights.

"I really don't know what I'm doing with you here in my hotel room. This wasn't in the plan," she admitted. "I just—had a really rough month before coming here."

"Plans are meant to be adjusted." He took off his shoes and made himself comfortable sitting up on the bed against the pillows. "Come and sit with me," he beckoned, his arms outstretched. "I have no ill will, I promise you."

She crawled onto the bed and he pulled her into his chest once again. "Sometimes, it just helps to have a friend."

"Don't you ever get lonely?" she asked. "You don't have a wife?"

He shook his head.

"Girlfriend?"

He shook his head.

"Boyfriend?" Her forehead crinkled with the last question.

This time he laughed. "No, I assure you I like women."

"I mean, it's a fair question."

"Yes. Yes, it is. You are right. The bigger question, I suppose, is why I don't have a woman in my life, and the answer is probably the same as yours. This life that we have chosen doesn't allow for anything sustainable."

That included Trevor as well, and Abby knew it. She sat up and crossed her legs, addressing him. "So, what is it you do in Spain for the other six months when you aren't leading tours?"

"I have many properties, in many regions of Spain. I visit them in Argentina's off-season to check in on things and handle my business affairs."

"Ok. That's interesting. So even when you're not leading tours, you're still riding a motorcycle and traveling?"

"Yes."

"What kind of properties? Businesses or rental homes?"

"Both, but businesses mostly. Restaurants and retail shops, and a couple of large grocery stores. Not large by American standards, but large by Spanish standards."

A couple of large grocery stores? "Basically, you do this for fun," she said, remembering the large stack of bills he'd pulled out of his pocket as if it was nothing.

"Basically." He smiled.

Everyone had an angle, but she hadn't deciphered his yet. "So you're *choosing* not to be in a relationship."

"I am *choosing* to do what I love. Not being able to be in a sustainable relationship is a consequence of that choice, not a choice in itself. There is a difference."

"Still. A Spaniard who chooses against love? That's got to be rare."

"Who said I was choosing against anything? I am not against being in love. I am happy with my life. I just have yet to find a woman who would make me want to choose differently."

"Now there's something we can agree on."

"What? You too are looking for the perfect woman?" He winked playfully.

She pushed his shoulder. "No. And perfection doesn't exist."

"You are right. But I don't mean what you think I mean. When I say perfect, I don't mean flawless. I mean authentically, beautifully flawed, like the jagged mountains or the raging sea. Perfection is in the eye of the beholder."

He was right, of course. In the States, perfection meant skinny models with long legs and boob jobs and picket fences surrounding manicured lawns. Even with all the time she spent away from it, those were still the images that flooded her mind and heart when she thought about it. It was wrong and she knew it, but silencing those voices was still difficult at times.

"Where I come from, perfect is—well, it's not flawed, and beauty? I suppose it all depends on how you look at it."

"But just think about the possibilities." He reached for her face and held it in his hands. "What if it was both?" He looked at her eyes, her lips, then he turned his gaze away.

"I must say, you show an amazing amount of restraint." Abby lay back, holding herself up on her elbows.

"It is my mother's fault."

"Your mother?"

"My mother made me promise that I would respect women, always, no matter what. That I would never look at their bodies as something I thought I could possess, but rather, something to appreciate and take pleasure in."

"Well, that's very honorable, but you're still human, aren't you?"

"I assure you I am very human. More so than I would like." Juan laughed. "My mother and I, we would stand in museums together staring at paintings and sculptures. She taught me to appreciate the beauty of a woman's form, and never to take it for granted. How marvelously put together they are." He sighed contentedly, as if even the memory brought him joy.

His hand gestured the shape of her curves without touching her. "The ability to give life and feed it." His eyes moved to her breasts. "The softness of your skin." He reached the back of his finger out and brushed her cheek ever so gently. "For this entire day, I have been a man at war with myself, which is why I stayed away from you at the spa."

"And now?" she asked.

"I am still a man at war. But now I know too much about you to treat this casually. I like you very much, but I am also a realist. We could take pleasure in one another, but I would want more, and neither of us has more to give. If I took from you—if I treated you like a *thing*—I would not only be disrespecting you, but I would also lose respect for myself in the process. I won't take from you."

Abby shook her head in disbelief. "Your mother must be a powerful woman." It was refreshing to hear someone speak with such respect for their mother. It was also sexy as hell.

"She was." He lay back and crossed his hands behind his head, looking up at the ceiling. "God rest her soul."

"I'm sorry," Abby whispered. "When did she die?"

"It's been a few years, but I still think about her every day. For so long, it was just the two of us. My father died when I was small."

"I lost both my parents at one time, in an accident, a little over three years ago."

He reached for her hand and their fingers intertwined.

"Everyone said time would heal, and that it would get easier." Abby sighed. "But it doesn't. The pain just dulls and forms into a sort of codified lump."

"I guess we are more alike than we realized."

Abby didn't possess his self-control, though she respected the shit out of him for it. On the one hand, she probably would have slept with him, had things played out differently. On the other, it was a relief not to have to navigate the rocky waters of a one-night stand. She felt oddly safe with this stranger, and it was nice.

"How would it be if we just held one another?" It was like he could read her mind. "It seems we could both use the comfort and warm arms of a friend." He released her hand and opened his arms.

She settled into his chest and the last thing she remembered was his hand gently caressing her hip. Soon they were fast asleep.

They both woke in the wee hours of the morning, just as light was breaking over the hills.

"I'm going to my room, Abby, to get some more sleep and a shower." He leaned over and kissed her forehead. "Will you have breakfast with me?"

She blinked a few times, trying to remember exactly where she was and what happened. She looked at Juan, then looked down at herself, still fully clothed.

"You are adorable when you're disoriented, do you know this?" He smiled. "And no, we did not have sex. We were not even drunk."

She rubbed the sleep out of her eyes and sat up. "Yet you want to have breakfast with me?"

He laughed. "Yes. As a matter of fact, I do. Get some more sleep. Let's meet at nine."

"Ok." She lay back down on the pillow and he covered her with the blankets. "Isn't nine a bit early for breakfast with a Spaniard?"

He came around to her side of the bed and set the alarm for eight thirty, just in case. "Not when he's meeting an American who has things to do at lunchtime. He will take what he can get. Now sleep." He kissed her forehead again and left.

Abby woke up on her own again around seven and used the bathroom. She showered and dressed and organized a few things. There were a few emails to return, but so far no one from today's group was having major issues with travel.

She thought about Juan. How warm and comfortable she felt with him, as if they were already fast friends that had shared similar joys and heartaches. If reincarnation were a real thing—and it seemed about as good an explanation as any—then maybe their souls had known each other in another life.

Suddenly the alarm clock rang, and she vaguely remembered Juan setting it before he left the room. Memories of Trevor tucking her into her bed in a similar fashion crept into her heart and pricked at its edges. It was easier to put him out of her mind while she was on tour, but he was always there, lurking in the background, even with a wonderful man like Juan vying for her attention.

It wasn't fair. After fifteen years of being relatively free, Trevor haunted her thoughts. Everything had come flooding back and soaked through her, bogging her down and making it harder to go through the motions of a life she thought she had figured out.

She went downstairs early to get a cup of coffee and figure out how to handle the inevitable goodbye. To her surprise, Juan was already sitting in the restaurant.

"What are you smiling about?" she asked as she approached the table.

"I woke up in my room thinking maybe last night was all a dream—that perhaps only in my dream did you agree to meet me for breakfast, but here you are!" He stood to seat her.

"That is one smooth line, I gotta tell you."

"It is the truth. Scout's honor." He held up three fingers, grinning.

"Where on earth did you learn that?" Abby laughed.

A devious grin flashed across his face. "American television, of course!"

The waiter poured her some coffee and brought a basket of bread and a plate of meats, cheeses, and jams. They spent a leisurely hour or so swapping more stories of travel and adventure, laughing and drinking coffee. By ten thirty she was looking at her watch.

"What are we going to do about this, Abby?"

"About what?"

"I want to see you again." He reached across the table and took her hand. "But we are going our separate ways." He rubbed his thumb across her wrist. "I have so enjoyed meeting you and beginning to get to know you. I want more."

Abby could see the sadness in his smile. "Seems to be an occupational hazard. Or at least, an unfortunate consequence of the lives we've chosen."

"It *is* unfortunate. I can honestly say, I don't meet very many people I feel this strongly about, this quickly. And before you protest, that is *not* a line to get you into bed. If I was going to try that, I would have done it last night," he joked.

"If you would have tried last night, I probably would have taken you up on it." Abby winked.

"*Now* you tell me!" He rolled his eyes playfully, then turned serious. "Listen to me, last night I told you that if we took pleasure in one another I would only end up wanting more, and yet neither of us has more to give."

Abby nodded. She remembered wondering if he was the only man on the planet who didn't think with his dick.

"Now I find myself in this unfortunate circumstance, where I still want more, and we didn't even have sex." He threw his hands up in mock disgust.

"Plus, now you're running the risk that I might, in fact, be a crappy lover."

"That's a really good point. I mean, life is too short to be sleeping with bad lovers," Juan agreed.

"Tell you what. I'll still be here one more night. You could stop by later and I could show you just how terrible I am in bed, and that could be the end of it." She put her hands up. "Put you out of your misery."

"You would do that, for me?" He placed both hands over his heart and feigned gratitude.

"I mean, if it would help." It was like a scene from *Seinfeld*, both of them playing their parts.

The waiter came over to refresh their coffee, but Abby put her hand over her cup, speaking Spanish to the waiter. Juan just leaned back in his seat shaking his head. "You didn't tell me you were fluent." This time he spoke Spanish to her.

"You didn't ask," she answered in his native tongue. "If you had struck up a conversation with me in Spanish on the bus, you would have known. You spoke English, so I did too." Then she finished, in English, "Besides, I'm not fluent."

"But you're very good." He pushed his plate away. "You know, I keep trying to find reasons not to be so attracted to you, but you're not making it easy on me."

"I know how you feel." She looked into his deep brown eyes for an extra moment, taking a mental picture, like Trevor did, of this man who was a mystery to her. "But I also agree with you. I think we should be happy that we met one another, and we should keep in touch. Who knows? Maybe our paths will cross again one day, maybe here or even in Spain." She smiled softly. "But it can't be more than that. We know it can't."

Juan sighed. "You are right, my dear Abby. You are right."

Abby started giggling. "Did you get that reference from American television too?"

"Get what?"

"*Dear Abby* was a syndicated newspaper column that gave advice to people who would write in with their questions."

Juan looked perplexed. "What kind of questions?"

"Oh, you know, like *Dear Abby, I love my husband, but the spark is gone from our marriage, what do I do?* Or maybe *Dear Abby, I was going through my son's drawers and found his dirty magazines. I want to talk to him, but I don't want him to know I was snooping through his things.*"

Juan started laughing. "Ok I've got one. How about this: *Dear Abby, I met someone recently while I was traveling. We really hit it off, but we live on opposite sides of the world and both travel all the time for work. I really think this could be something deep and meaningful if we let it, but neither one of us is willing to give up our traveling lifestyle. What should I do?*" Juan smiled softly.

He had deftly worked the truth directly into their banter and it stopped her cold. "I don't know what to say." It was an impossible situation, which was why it was usually easier not to feel anything. Maybe having a one-night stand and calling it good for another month or two would have been the better part of valor. A relationship would be impossible to maintain. And then there was the whole Trevor situation.

"You don't have to say anything," he added. "I am just stating the obvious."

"I can't afford distractions."

"I know. Let's change the subject." He slapped both hands on the table. "Tell me about these women who come on your tours."

"They're all different."

"From the US, mostly?"

"About—seventy percent, I'd say. But women from other countries come too. This time, I have one woman from Brazil and two from Denmark."

"So, now that I know that you are the boss, tell me—why not open a tour to men as well as women?"

"Three reasons." Abby held up her fingers. "The first is that straight men tend to want to show off in front of women. They generally won't listen to directions from a woman, and they end up doing things that are either stupid or put others in danger. Having them in the same group rarely works out well."

Juan nodded. "Many men have a certain need to impress the targets of our attraction. But not all of us are like that."

"True, but you don't get to pick and choose on a tour like this. The first reason plays into the second. I'm not a camp counselor or a dating service, and the whole drama of people hooking up on the tours is something I just can't deal with, which is also why I have really strict rules about drinking and riding."

"Ok, but what if two women want to hook up?"

"It happens, but they tend to be more discreet, and so far, it's been fairly drama-free. I had one couple who met on one of my tours and then came back to do another location with me as an anniversary celebration of how they met. It was really cool."

"And the third reason?"

Abby got quiet. "My tours aren't like a lot of the other ones."

"What does that mean?"

"Steel Journeys is a metaphor for a motorcycle, of course,

but also for the solid base of strength a woman needs to complete her own personal journey through life."

"So, what? On the first night you smoke peyote and help them find their life path?"

"No! Although, I did that once. It was some pretty powerful shit."

Juan's eyebrows went up. "That's a story I would also like to hear some time."

"I guess I've just—learned to ask the right questions. I mean, I was searching once too. Searching for big answers to hard questions. Most people who carve out the money and the time to do something like this are here because they're looking for a piece of themselves that they lost along the way, or maybe they weren't sure if it was ever really there in the first place."

"I don't mean to sound rude but, what does that have to do with you?" Juan asked.

"Each day, we focus on a progressively deeper level of questioning. We start out getting to know one another on the surface. Then, the questions go deeper. We start to uncover and share the answers to questions I've written out beforehand."

"Like homework?" He asked.

"They get a new question each day at breakfast, have time to think and talk about them with one another throughout the day, and then each evening at dinner we spend time sharing our answers. Over the course of our week or ten days together, we build a real and deep sense of community and support."

"Why do you choose to do it that way? Why not just lead the motorcycling part of it and let them figure out the rest on their own?"

"I guess it's because I believe strongly in the power of human connection and interaction," Abby said. "As humans we were made for depth, and yet most people live at surface level only. They know things *about* other people, but they don't really ever get to *know* other people. Each of these tours makes a true impact on these women's lives. We share stories and fears, laughter, and tears, and I'm not sure that would fly in a group where men and women were mixed. So that's the third reason."

Juan sat across from her, wordless, his eyes gentle but full of deep thoughts.

"This format I've developed is part tour guide, part life coach, and I think in some ways this...strength of authentic connection, is how I choose to cope with the loneliness of this lifestyle." As the words poured out of her mouth, the realization became clear, and it was a truth she had never spoken aloud. She wasn't even sure she'd ever admitted it to herself.

"I've never met anyone like you. Ever." Juan's eyes narrowed slightly, as if it could help him to see her even more clearly.

She leaned her elbows on the table and Juan reached for her hands. "That sounds incredible, Abby. I have to say, it makes what I do—leading tours of mostly men who drink and smoke too much and tell half-truths about their conquests, seem quite shallow by comparison."

She smiled as he released her hands. "I assure you, that was not my intention."

"I know, and I'm trying to pay you a compliment. I think you are doing a great thing. You are changing people's lives."

"I love my job." Abby nodded in agreement. "Honestly? I wouldn't trade it for anything."

"Not even a fancy house on the Mediterranean Sea?" He winked.

"Is that an invitation? Or are you pitching me one of your rental properties?"

"You have an open invitation to stay at any of my houses in Spain, any time you wish, whether I am there or not." He slid a business card in her direction. It had a number handwritten across the front of it. "We never did exchange information, so here is mine. This number is my personal cell. I hope you will take me up on my offer, one of these days."

"Which offer is that?" Abby slipped the card into her pocket and pulled out one of hers. "I'd love to. Spain is a beautiful country, and the riding there is fantastic."

"It is," he agreed. "Perhaps you could take a couple of weeks to ride with me some time, and I will show you my country in a way you have never seen it before."

"I just might take you up on that."

"I have many bikes for you to choose from."

"Many?"

"Six or seven, I guess."

Six or seven? She glanced down at his name on the card and decided to Google him later. "I have to get going, but I want to thank you."

"For what?"

"For being such a gentleman, for your wonderful company, and for holding me last night, even though you didn't have to."

"The pleasure has been mine, Abby Steel." Juan stood as she stood, reached for her hand, and kissed it, bowing slightly.

She leaned in and kissed his cheek. "Thank you for breakfast. I'll be in touch."

Juan simply nodded once and smiled back.

Something about walking away from Juan turned her thoughts once again toward Trevor. Men like Juan and Trevor were rare, and under different circumstances, either one of them might have tempted her away from her passions and caused her to settle for less than everything.

Abby walked out the front door to wait for the shuttle that would take her to Temuco, where she would retrieve the nine other women who were coming for the tour.

Every time she thought about slowing her life down, she couldn't help but think about all the fascinating people she would miss. Like Elena, a woman from Argentina with a head for business, and Juan—a gentleman from Spain who shared her passion for motorcycles. Or Mia—a woman who owned an inn near the sea in Chile and would welcome her with open arms.

For all of its wars and famine and natural disasters and threats of terrorism, it was still a beautiful world full of wonderful people. Being continually reminded of that soothed her pain, pulling her focus away from her own internal struggles and giving her a broader perspective on humanity.

Traveling had changed her. It helped her to understand that her own troubles were not so large and looming by comparison and helped her to see things from a completely different perspective. It gave her wings.

It was time to put away thoughts of the men who jockeyed for space in her heart. It was time for another adventure.

The End

REVIEWS / NEWSLETTER

Leave a Review

Thanks for reading *Steel Journeys*! Your support makes it possible for this independent author to continue creating.

If you liked what you read, please **leave an honest review** wherever you bought this book! Your feedback really is invaluable.

Newsletter

I send out a newsletter with updates once a month, and they're packed full of news, updates, and **unpublished writing that you, my subscribers get first!**

I don't sell or give your email to any third parties, nor do I use them for any other purposes.

Just updates. You have my word.

Sign up here:

http://createdtofly.com/**newsletter**/

ABOUT THE AUTHOR

Lynda Meyers is an award-winning author, nurse, yoga instructor, reiki master, motorcycle enthusiast and world traveler. She has written fiction, non-fiction and poetry for newspapers and magazines and currently makes her home in the upper left corner of the United States.

Steel Journeys: The Road to Patagonia is her fourth book.

To learn more, visit: www.createdtofly.com

LYNDA
MEYERS

the
truth
about
truly

The companion novel to *Finn Again*

THE TRUTH ABOUT TRULY

BY: LYNDA MEYERS

She was the girl of his dreams.

It was a chance meeting, but Finn knew her at a glance. The likeness was unmistakable. Even her smell was familiar.

The problem was, Truly wasn't looking for love.

When Truly loved someone, it was a death sentence—and she wasn't going to have that on her conscience. Not again. Love and death were partners in crime, and she couldn't risk doing any more time.

Finn wasn't willing to give up. He'd cheated death twice in Afghanistan. Three times if you count nearly drowning in whiskey and painkillers. He'd been through scores of women, but had loved only once—until now.

His dreams didn't lie: this girl was his destiny. He needed to woo her. He needed to win her heart—*if he could just manage to stay alive.*

She wasn't looking for a knight in shining armor.

He wasn't looking for a beauty to rescue.

But one fateful night changed all that. For both of them.

LYNDA
MEYERS

finn
again

The long-awaited prequel to *The Truth About Truly*

DESCRIPTION: FINN AGAIN

Read the Prequel to The Truth About Truly:

Finn Again

Finn McCarthy is half Irish, half English, and fully fantastic.

Raised in the pubs and educated at Oxford, he never did know which half to favor. His Irish half loves women and booze, while his English half is wicked smart and damned polite. And then there's Regan, the one girl who never did succumb to his charms.

When a world at war beckons, Finn answers the call, but there are some casualties even a soldier can't prepare for. To heal his wounds he must banish his demons, a journey that leads him to a sleepy fishing village where the mysteries of his Celtic roots take hold. He begins to accept his past, only to discover that his greatest battle might take everything he's got left.

War...Does things to a man. But Finn isn't just any man.

LYNDA
MEYERS

Letters
from
the
Ledge

LETTERS FROM THE LEDGE

Still reeling from the suicide of his best friend Tess, seventeen-year old Brendan struggles to overcome addiction and identity issues. Walking the ledge outside his Manhattan apartment has become its own sort of drug, as he stands night after night with his arms outstretched, ready to fly away.

Sarah can see him from her window and begins journaling about a boy on a ledge. Paige and Nate, a young couple in another building, can see both teens from their fire escape.

None of them know the others are watching, but a strong desire for freedom resides in each of them, and as their lives begin to intertwine, that desire will be tested.

Three buildings. One city block. Three stories. One common thread.

Sharp, humorous, and deeply layered, this chronicle of a suicidal teen's survival explores the reality of addiction and other tough issues, but does so easily, through the use of multiple perspectives, intelligent dialogue and authentic characters. Equal parts romance, contemporary drama, and coming of age, this highly engaging and intensely beautiful novel challenges our cultural perceptions in the battle for balance, deftly uncovering the hopes, dreams and fears that keep us from falling, and ultimately teach us how to fly.

Made in the USA
San Bernardino, CA
19 November 2019